D1529146

The Roamer

Benjamin Jenum

Amazon Kindle Direct Publishing

ALSO BY BENJAMIN JENUM

*=UNPUBLISHED

Ben's Journal*
2013–2016

My Father's Reckoning*
2020

The Cavern of Cawdorn*
2021

The Vagabond
2022

Missing In Montana
2023

Whisked Away (with Rachel Trettin)
2024

Dedication

For Grandpa Ron, the character "Raynold," one of my best friends, who always loved when I would write books. ♥ I love you forever.

1946-2024

Copyright

Foreword

I have been writing books since the COVID-19 pandemic shuttered everyone into their homes. I have so many ideas and stories that I have come up with since then that I badly want to tell, but coming up with solid storylines and details to make it happen can be really challenging. I remember when I finally finished my first real book in December 2020. My grandpa - Ron Penberthy - texted me asking how he could get an autographed copy of my book. Me, being very self-conscious about my first book, had only one copy made and did not want that book to get into distribution. However, I still remember his excitement and pride at knowing that his grandson had actually written a book, and could be considered an "author." Fast forward another year or two, I wrote another book that I was comfortable with distributing, and of course, Grandpa Ron was the first one on the list. Not long after, I got a text saying that he finished the book, saying "You are definitely an AUTHOR!" You knew it was written by Grandpa Ron if at least some of what he said was written in all capital letters. From then on, he became sort of a sounding board for listening to my many other story ideas. I sometimes would joke with him that he was such a little hooligan when he was younger, his life would provide a great opportunity to write a story around. I don't know if he ever took me too seriously, but the story you are about to read is that story. "Raynold Penfield" is my grandfather. The story is a highly fictionalized version of part of his life growing up. It does contain tidbits of real information and maybe some "Easter eggs," that our family will hopefully be able to pick out, as well. I decided to hit the gas on this story because Grandpa developed a love for reading later in life – and you will find out soon that one of the last things Raynold Penfield would ever do at his age would be to pick up a book and read it. I was truly hoping that one day, I would be able to reward Grandpa by giving him a book to read where he is the central character. Most regrettably, it was not meant to be. Grandpa Ron had been fighting health issues with his eyes, ears, and legs for some time already, years prior to me even beginning my journey writing books. However, I do recall the phone call with him (while he was in a hospital), when I told him that I am going to write a story with him as the main character, and I needed his help making the characters' personalities as accurate as possible. He gave his best effort at providing as much information as he possibly could, and he was especially helpful in helping me craft the image of his mother, who actually did pass away when Grandpa was around this age. Regrettably, by the time I finished this story, Grandpa himself succumbed to his ailments. The strokes, infections, arthritis, and neuropathy had become too much for his body to handle. His eyesight was nearly gone, his hearing was only somewhat there if he had hearing aids in, and he could no longer walk. So, after he died, I made it a number one priority to finish this book, in order to dedicate it to his memory. We are talking about somebody who was such a supporter of my book writing adventures and so many other things throughout the time he was in my life. I miss him terribly every day. But, I pray he would enjoy this story if he were to read it, and would think to himself "Yep! I can see myself as that guy! Ben really nailed it!"

I want to extend a special thanks to MaryLou, Julie, and Kevin, Grandpa's siblings, for the additional information that was given to me that helped me write this story. I appreciate all of you very much.

The Roamer

The Roamer

Chapter One

"*Raynold!*" I hear shouted from across the house. "Raynold! Get moving! You'll be late for your lesson!"

I sulk. I don't want to go. I don't want to play the trombone. I don't want to move. I don't want to do anything today. Tomorrow isn't looking real promising either. It's a beautiful winter morning. The last thing I want to do is spend it cooped up in some old man's house learning to play an instrument that I am mediocre at, at best. *"First position, third position, blow harder, do this, do that!"* My teacher's voice buzzes in my head like a mosquito.

No. On cold days like today, I wish I could spend the first part in bed, wrapped with a blanket over me, nice and warm. My mom would come in, pat me on the head, put another blanket over me, and then she'd say...

"LET'S GO, RAYNOLD! GET MOVING! I'M NOT GOING TO CALL YOU AGAIN!"

Well, okay. Not that. But that would be the first part of the day. After that, I would run outside after lunch, go sledding, sneak around through town, and goof off until it was dark outside. That's how I like to spend my weekends when I'm not slaving away in school. But, today...today I am going to be stuck inside Mr. Saar's centuries-old brick house, full of decorations that would break if you so much as breathed on them. On days like today, I am tempted to purposefully mess it up, just so he'll say I'm hopeless, there's no sense in trying to teach someone like me, and then I can be free. But, my parents insist that I must play an instrument. So, here I sit.

Not to mention, it's not my mom that's hollering. It's my dad. Unfortunately, my mom hasn't even been able to walk, let alone yell across the house, for quite some time. She's battling cancer - and it's terminal. That said, it's mainly Mom that wants me to play an instrument, and I don't want to disappoint her. According to Dad and the doctors, the cancer is slowly destroying her insides. She hasn't been around much lately with how much she's been in the hospital. That means my dad has had to step it up quite a bit. Lately, it seems that most of his attention goes toward my youngest brother, Keith. Unless, of course, he's yelling at me to get my butt moving to my trombone lesson, like today.

Purposefully moving as slow as possible, I drag myself out of bed and put my clothes on. I want so badly to just be carefree and goof off today. But no matter how much I beg my dad, he won't cave.

"Get moving," he grouches. "I'll need you to walk today since I need to take Keith to get his haircut before I visit your mom."

Sighing, I salute him and goose-step out the door. My sisters are self-sufficient enough, for the most part anyway. They have each other. But me? I am on my own. With Dad directing most of his energy toward Keith, and Mom being laid up, who is there to raise me?

Lugging my instrument case through the brisk air and deep snow, I purposefully take as long a time getting there as I possibly can. When I finally walk up Mr. Saar's driveway, he isn't smiling.

"You're late," he grouches. "I'll have to let your father know about this. Come on in, quickly," he mutters without looking at me.

Taking my usual seat near the window with the music stand in front of it, I get everything ready to play. Reluctantly, I let him lead me through every boring song in the book. I swear this book is meant for little kids. They have no good songs in there. It would be nice if there was some Elvis music in this book. I don't know why I'm wasting my time coming in today.

"It's clear to me you aren't spending much time practicing, Penfield," he drones slowly and mournfully. "Fix it by next week. By then, I expect perfection. If you want these lessons to be done, I suggest you start to put some effort into these."

Slapping my head with the book, he tells me to pack up and get out of here. He doesn't need to tell me twice, I hate going to trombone lessons, if that isn't clear already.

Making sure he is no longer looking, I give him the finger and walk away, and "accidentally" knock over the snowman his grandson made. I am just far enough away to hear him yell at me from his porch door. I run like the wind.

The Roamer

.ₘᴹₖ.

When I get back onto our property, eager to be inside, I run past Dad and away from the trouble I had likely gotten myself into. If I were more observant, I might have noticed the snow shovel in his one hand, and his other hand on his hip.

I throw my instrument into my bedroom and go downstairs. I am surprised to find Mom at home in the living room. She is almost never home anymore - her health has gotten so bad, she constantly needs the attention of every doctor in existence, it seems. Though I would never say it out loud, especially not to Dad, the way Mom looks scares me to death. She is thin - skeletal, really, and looks nothing like the mom I remember from when I was a really little kid. Her eyes are sinking into her head, her hair is thinning, her abdomen is bloated, and she can't really walk anymore without help due to being in such tremendous pain. She has been like this for the past few months. Though it hurts, I don't like to be around her. Not that I don't love her, I absolutely do. But she's not the same Mom that I remember. I want to remember her as she was, not as she is right now. Though I am aware of the possibility - I don't want to consider it - but I know it is possible that she may never recover from this.

I make myself go over there to say hello. My sisters and brother are nowhere in sight, nor is Dad, which is especially peculiar. She is sitting in her recliner, breathing low and labored, barely registering that I am right next to her. It scares me to do so, but I put my hand on hers. Soon, she opens her eyes and sees me. She smiles, and squeezes my hand. "How's my Ray?" she asks me sweetly, but hoarsely. I feel tears welling up in my eyes, but I force them back. I won't cry, no way. I am too old for that. I have to be tough. Though it's hard, I squeeze her hand back and say I am good, as she asks me how school is going.

I don't say anything back. It wouldn't do any good to tell her that my grades are awful, and I am constantly getting into trouble for cutting up in class. Heck, I had just purposefully failed a trombone lesson and had irritated my teacher just fifteen minutes ago. But, I know Mom wants me to do well in school, and I don't want her to be disappointed in me, especially not when she's like this.

I guess I waited too long, though. My silence tells her the

truth.   "Ray, you must try to do better.   You must get your work done and respect your teachers.   A good education is important.   You must – "

She was interrupted by a coughing fit.   Harsh, low, loose coughs – from deep within her.   She puts her hanky up to her mouth to cough into, and when she is finally done, I am startled to see bright red blood.   She notices it too, but doesn't seem to be affected by it, as if this is normal, and she knows what is happening to her.

"Like I was saying, try harder in school.   Get your homework done. Don't give the teachers any trouble. If there's anything you could do for me, it's that. Please, Ray. Just try."

She barely gets that out before coughing even harder.   Fortunately, there is no more blood this time.

The Roamer

I sigh. "I promise," I say. And Lord, I hope I can keep it. There is no telling just how hard it is going to be to keep my word, especially when my pals and I get together. It's so easy to horse around and goof off. But, I made a promise to Mom that I would try hard, and I will.

॰॰॰

Right then, Dad walks in. He had been outside shoveling snow. "Ray!" he barks. "Where were you? You think Keith is old enough to do this? I could've used your help, you know!"

"Sorry," I mumble. "I was talking to Mom." Indifferent to me, he goes right on talking, barely hearing me.

"You've been so damn lazy lately!" he goes on. "Cutting up in school, shirking your chores, neglecting every simple responsibility I give you, making me do everything around here when I work full time, and have four kids to provide for, most of whom don't care or don't realize all I'm doing. It gets damn old, son, damn old!" He is shouting now, and Mom's eyes have closed again, I'm sure barely registering what is happening. She gets tired easily, so easily.

"I just got back from trombone! Then I saw Mom, and I was just talking with her, that's all. I wasn't trying to – "

"Bull!" says Dad, jabbing a finger at me, poking me hard in the chest. "You ran right by me as you got home. Now get upstairs and do your homework!"

He scowls at me the entire way as I sulk upstairs, purposefully going as slow as possible. I just can't please him, no matter what. I want to make Dad happy, but he's always angry about something. His thankless, full-time, low-paying job, my sisters making noise, Keith leaving his toys laying around, the doctors not doing enough for Mom, me cutting up and failing classes in school...it's always something. It never ends. I genuinely can't remember the last time I have seen Dad happy.

Drudging through my schoolwork, I scuttle through as much of it as I can, dreading getting it back after it's graded, knowing it will never satisfy Dad.

᙮ᙗᙘᙡ

A few days later, Mom goes back to the hospital after falling in the bathroom. For some sad reason, I get this terrible gut feeling that she won't be back after this one. But, I can hope for the best.

At school, I am sitting at the lunch table with my two best buddies, my only true friends, Gordy and Greg. We have been friends since kindergarten, and always had each others' backs. The amount of times we have gotten into trouble together, driven the teachers insane, and skipped class, are absolutely countless. "The Three Musketeers" is our reputation among the teachers, one that we wear like a badge of honor.

"Hey, what are your plans this weekend?" I ask both of them, hoping they will tell me something fun they have in mind that will help me keep my mind off of my parents for a little bit.

Greg takes a bite of broccoli and washes it down with a swallow of milk. "I got homework," he says, followed by Gordy echoing him. "Me too, my mom will kill me if I keep missing assignments."

I eat the last bite of my hotdog, hoping they will smile and grin at me, like they are kidding. But they don't.

"Come on, guys, what gives? You barely do any homework, why now? We always screw around before we do any homework, if we even do it at all. And besides, I'm desperate to get away from my house. My dad and sisters are driving me crazy. Can't we just sneak into the church basement and goof around for a bit?"

They exchange a look with each other that I don't particularly like, as if they are communicating in a language they don't want me to understand. Without answering me, they just go right back to their lunch.

I start to get angry. Standing up, I almost holler at them. "Why don't you say what you mean?! What gives? Am I suddenly not good enough for you? That's what it is, isn't it? You think you're better than me now all of a sudden?"

Looking scared, they cower back. "No, Ray...no. That's not it...it's just..."

"Just what?" I say after a pause. "Just that you don't like my dad, you feel weird around my mom, and my sisters are annoying? Is that why you don't want to be around me all of a sudden?"

"Of course not, Ray. We're just busy, that's all." Getting up, they walk toward the garbage can, and walk outside together, leaving me behind. That's that.

The rest of that day, they don't say anything to me, but they stick tight to each other, seeming to not remember that I'm their friend too, at least I was not too long ago. It tortures me to think of why they are turning their backs on me...what did I ever do to them? They seem to be turning into jerks, and there isn't a damn thing I can do about it.

I try telling myself that maybe they are just having a bad day, they can't really be avoiding me after all. But the next day is just the same, and the next, and the next. Throughout the next few days, my mom's health doesn't improve, nor does my dad's attitude, nor does the weather. It's still as cold and snowy as ever. I am going crazy in my own skin, and again, I can't do a single thing about it. The whole world seems to have an ax to grind with me.

~M~

One day in early February, I'm sitting in math class on a particularly cold and bitter day, bored out of my mind. At this exact moment I am daydreaming about hopping on a train and getting the heck out of Saint Paul. Where I'll go, I don't know, but anywhere would be better than here. My uncle owns a milk delivery business in Brainerd, and I have good memories during some of the summers when I was little of riding with him, and going house to house selling milk to families. Maybe he will take me in - after all, nobody else seems to care about me. Maybe I'll discover I am good at sales; maybe I can join him in the business after I turn 18. Of course I'm not sure about trading one cold Minnesota community for another, but of course, anything is better than the life I am currently living.

The Roamer

I'm daydreaming about what kind of milk salesman I'll be, and doodling on my notebook paper the kind of truck I'd be driving, when the teacher starts passing back the quizzes we took last week. I don't know what kind of grade I had been expecting to get, but it sure wasn't a "D." Groaning, I put my head down on my desk.

It's right then that I hear Greg, who is sitting right behind me, whisper to Gordy, who is sitting right across the aisle from him, something that makes my blood boil. He isn't expecting me to hear him, but I do.

"Hey Gordy. Skippy here wants to be a milk salesman but he's too dumb to multiply numbers that have more than one digit in each column. He'll get screwed in every deal if he sells milk the way he takes math quizzes." Gordy snickers with laughter.

I don't know if I'm more shocked at their bluntness, or boiling with anger, hearing one of my best friends talk about me like that, thinking I can't hear them.

Turning around, I twist my face so he'd know exactly how I felt about him in that instant. "What the hell did you say, you jerk?"

Greg is so shocked that I had heard him, he has nothing to say. I see pure shock in his eyes. "Ah – uh, nothing, Ray. Nothin' at all...I mean, I was just kid – "

Before he could finish his sentence, without thinking, I let my temper spill over. I finally tell him exactly what I think of all of his avoidance, small talk, and now, trash talk. I tell him with my fist, good and hard, right in the face.

The Roamer

Blood shoots out of his nose, his teeth go flying. Lord, I have never hit anyone so hard in my life. All my anger is spilling out. When the teacher pulls me off of him, there is so much pandemonium in class I think the room is about to explode. When I get another good look at him, his face is bloody, his shirt is ripped, blood pours from his nose, and he sports two black eyes. Boy, I am really in for it.

"What the hell are you doing, Penfield?!" the teacher shouts. Not only do I have the whole class's attention now, but teachers and kids peek in from the hallway, wondering what is going on.

I have nothing to say. Ignoring all of his questions, I let him drag me away toward the principal's office. If I know Mr. Tobias at all, he'll call my father, and he'll have to come pick me up for a few days of suspension.

This is how my life is going. I have friends turning on me. I have awful grades. I have a dying mother who is probably ashamed of me. And now, I will have a furious father who will have nothing kind to say to me. My life feels like one giant disappointment. And I am going to have to face my father, whether I want to or not.

I sit in the office with the secretary, Mrs. James. Fortunately, she is nice, and looks at me with empathy. Even though I don't have much to say, it's nice to be with somebody who doesn't want blood from me.

When my father walks into the office, I'm expecting him to come in birds flying, angry, shouting, cussing me out. It's what he does at home, and he had to leave work early to come get me from class after I started a fight. His job doesn't pay him anywhere near what he is worth to them, so it's not likely they will be paying him to come get his kid who is cutting up.

But to my huge surprise, he doesn't even look angry when he walks in. He comes in with a sullen, defeated, tired look on his face. He moves slower and less confidently; he doesn't have his usual swagger. He also doesn't give off his usual intimidating vibe. I know something is wrong.

"I'm here to pick up Raynold," he says softly to Mrs. James. I approach him gingerly, hoping that his calm demeanor isn't just a facade, and he isn't a bomb waiting to explode.

Mrs. James hands Dad my folders containing the homework I'd be missing, and Mr. Tobias stares at us sternly with his arms crossed from his office doorway. Dad doesn't even acknowledge him.

When we get to the car, he still hasn't said a word to me. By the time he gets the car started and we get onto the road, I can't take the anticipation of the explosion anymore. I speak to him.

"Dad, I'm sorry, I lost my temper. My friends were trash-talking me. I didn't mean to make you go to this trouble. I - "

He holds up his hand at me. The set of his back and the way he grips the steering wheel tell me that this is not a good time to talk to him.

When we get home, I walk into the house, only to be faced with my sisters and brother crying on the

couch.   Dad throws his cap down
and walks downstairs. The whole
house has an eerie, sad, heavy
feeling to it.

"What is it?" I manage to
choke out. My older sister, Mary
Lynn, looks up as if she has just
noticed me. "It's Mom," she cries.
"Mom is dead."

Chapter Two

"NO!" I shout, immediately angry. I am dumb for not seeing it coming, in fact, in the back of my mind, I had...but now that the day is finally here, I can't take it. Mom is dead. The one person in the family that I knew I could trust and count on, is gone. What a stupid, stupid world.

This is it. I've had enough. This time, I am the one who throws down my instrument and chases after Dad. Now I am mad at him. He had just driven me the whole way home and didn't have the decency to so much as tell me what had happened. Not even a hint. Not a word.

I find him downstairs with a bottle of liquor in his hand. Before he knew what I was doing, I grab it from his grip, and smash it on the floor. Broken glass goes everywhere and the shattering bottle makes a loud noise in the small downstairs basement.

"HEY!" he shouts. "WHAT GIVES-" I jump in before he can finish. "WHY DIDN'T YOU TELL ME ABOUT MOM!" I scream over him. "WHY DID YOU JUST LEAVE IT TO ME TO FIND OUT ON MY OWN! YOU ALWAYS IGNORE ME. YOU ARE ALWAYS MAD AT ME. I HATE YOU! I WISH IT WAS YOU AND NOT MOM!"

Dad slaps me then. Grabbing me by the scruff of my shirt, he pulls me close, close enough to where I can smell the booze on his breath, and something less pleasant on his skin.

"Don't you yell at me, you little snot. You know how hard I work busting my ass to provide for this family? Only for miserable little ungrateful twerps like you to scream in my face? Show me some damn respect, son!" He is jabbing his index finger right into my face.

I pull away from him forcefully. "Respect you?! You're never here! I'm on my own! Mom has been sick, you're nowhere to be seen! What am I supposed to do? How am I supposed to show respect for someone who is supposed to be my leader when you don't lead anything at all! You're worthless!"

I am hitting him now. Hard, in the stomach. All the while, he is trying to pull me off of him, but I don't care. I want to smash things and fight. All of my pent-up anger is boiling over right in this moment. I feel the slightest bit badly when I realize that my siblings have come downstairs to see what the commotion is, but not bad enough to stop hitting Dad.

Finally, Dad has had enough. Grabbing me by my shoulders and shaking me roughly, he shoves me backwards against the wall, hard. Coming away from the wall, dizzy, I saw that he pushed me so hard that I made a hole in the wall with my body. He stands doubled over in pain in the center of the room, his eyes filled with hurt and rage. His face is a deep, angry shade of red. I know that what is about to come out of his mouth next is going to be anything but kind.

"Get. To. Your. Room." he growls at me through his teeth. I can hear his temper seething. His world is falling apart. He is losing control in real time. And I am at the point where I don't think I could care less.

"Good riddance!" I yell in his face as I barrel past my siblings on the steps. I took a bow at the top of the stairs for them, to show them just how much I think of their snooping. "Get a camera next time, all of you!" I shout.

In my room, I don't waste any time sitting on my bed. Slinging my duffel bag out of the closet, I pack as many clothes into it as I can, along with some paper, and, after some thought, my trombone.

Rushing back to the kitchen, I am also able to grab some oatmeal and a few bottles of Orange Nehi before Dad and my siblings show back up at the top of the basement steps.

"Don't you dare walk out of here!" he screams as I run down the sidewalk toward the road. "You need me! You won't last a second out there!"

I keep my pace and try to tune his angry voice out of my mind. The last I hear from him is him yelling *"Don't you even think about crawling back here when you find you can't make it, you hear?!"*

"Who needs you?!" is the last thing I shout before turning the corner toward the highway.

For a long while after, step after agonizing step along the highway, the sound of his angry voice sends echoes through my mind.

The Roamer

⠰⠒

I do not care where I am going and when I am going to stop. School be damned at this point. I can't stop thinking about Mom, and how I had just snapped on Dad. I feel the devil and the angel on both of my shoulders. The devil is telling me that I don't need my mom or my dad, that I could live just fine all by myself out here. Dad is an alcoholic who doesn't care, and Mom left us too soon, whether she chose to or not. My friends have turned their backs on me too. I've made it this far, haven't I? What's the rest of my life? I tell myself at this moment that I don't need anybody, not now, not ever. Taking stock again of the few items I brought with me, I walk on. It's me against the world at this point.

The Roamer

I walk, and walk, and walk, and walk well into the night until finally I cannot take another step. My mind and body will not let me go any further. I cannot tell where I am, but I don't recognize the surroundings, which tell me I have gone far enough for now. It strikes me, but I have never truly left my little bubble in St. Paul ever since I was born. I was born in Bemidji, but we moved to St. Paul when I was a toddler. Now, I am finally spreading my wings, for better or for worse. But for now, I'm stopping.

I park myself under a small picnic shelter and settle in as nicely as I can. It is far from comfortable, but it will do for a few hours. Freezing my rear end off, with lots on my mind, my tired brain finally lets me fall asleep for a short while.

In the morning, I don't spend much time getting ready for the day. I continue my journey as if my life depends on it, because to some extent, it does.

As I walk the streets of the cities, I begin to notice things that I never had experienced before. The buildings are so much taller than anything I've experienced in our little nook in St. Paul. Everything isn't so closed in by fences, bushes, and houses squeezing the life out of each other. The buildings are tall, people walk by in a rush, cars cruise by you on a mission. For a short while, I slow down and enjoy the change in scenery; Mom forgotten for a window in time.

Throughout this day and the next, I wander the streets. It's cold, that's what's most obvious everywhere I go. Every once in a while, the cold becomes too much and I hitchhike a ride for a few miles when I am too tired to walk. By the time the end of my second full day rolls around, I have eaten through my dry oatmeal and the Nehi is long gone. I'm starving and thirsty and would do anything for a drink of water. I have no money. If I want water or anything to eat, it's on me to find it on my own.

I go to bed shivering under a slide on a playground that night; listening to the grumbles of my stomach. My tongue feels like sandpaper after not drinking any water after walking nearly all day. It's not easy to sleep, and I know that if I'm going to last on this journey, then I need to get a new world order in place.

Somehow, I'm still not sure how, I manage to fall asleep that night. My stomach is growling something terrible for some real food, and my mouth feels disgusting; like it's crying out for water.

By now, I've reached a point where I am walking along a long stretch of highway, a car passing every few minutes. I hold my thumb out to each of them, hoping that one of them will take me out of the state, somewhere where I can just start over.

.^^^^.

Finally, a car slows down and indicates it is going to stop for me. Inside, I find a weathered looking man who looks like he's seen his better days. His car is a filthy rust bucket, making it look like it was made in the stone ages. As I get inside, I can barely sit down with my bag, due to all of the garbage he has piling up from the floor. My mom used to pick at me all the time for not keeping a clean room before she got sick; so I would usually pay my sister a dollar to do it for me. But, this car pales in comparison to anything my bedroom ever looked like. Moldy food on the floor, musty newspapers, beer bottles, cigarette butts, bugs, and dozens and dozens of old clothes. I almost vomit just from the smell. If I wasn't so desperate to find something to eat and drink, I wouldn't have gotten in.

The driver didn't look much better. His sweatshirt is shredded, he wears a faded, sweat-stained hat, his glasses are smudged, and the few teeth he does have are brown. His neck has what looks to be a permanent ring of dirt around it. He smells like some sick combination of alcohol, smoke, and sweat. Something in my head is telling me this guy is bad news – and I should not get in his car. But, I justify it by saying that I won't be riding with this guy real long – at least I sure hope not.

The first few minutes of the ride are spent in silence. I hold my breath as long as I can to keep from smelling what smells like rotting salmon coming from the back seat.

"Where you off too, kid? Shouldn't you be in school?" asks my driver.

Letting my breath out slowly, I answer "no place special. Just wherever my feet take me, I guess. I'll start with some place down South. But hopefully before then I'll land someplace where I can find a meal and some water."

He just nods.

I let some more silence go by before a burning question exits my lips. "Where exactly are YOU off to?

I think I'll get off at the next larger town. I'll find some water there."

What I really mean is, I am desperate to be out of this Dutch oven. It's freezing outside but in here I feel like I'm going to roast just from this man's fumes. My eyes are watering from the smell of this car.

Suddenly, the man starts to chuckle. "I think you may have made a mistake here, kid. You have no idea just how long I've been waiting for a moment like this. You and I are going South, alright. But we're off to Mexico."

My heart starts pumping into my head. As soon as he starts chuckling and talking, I realize I have just made a tremendous mistake.

"Mexico?" I say, trying to still sound tough. "Why there? Why me? Get me out of here!"

"SHUT UP!" he screams, scaring the living hell out of me. He looks at me with such a fierce, terrifying face, I swear the devil himself has just walked in and possessed him. Before I can say anything more, he looks forward, and lets out a terrifying and guttural scream – and my insides shake with fear as we continue down the road.

<u>*Chapter Three*</u>

I am petrified. No longer thinking or caring about my hunger or thirst, I begin thinking of what I am going to do to escape. Suddenly I am faced with the realization - I have made a huge mistake. Even being with my alcoholic father seems better than being in here with this unstable, insane, disgusting freak.

He continues cackling at nothing and nobody in particular. I swear he has even forgotten that I am in the car. I just sit there - terrified - wondering what he is going to do with me.

Beforelong, he pulls into a gas station. Right as I am about to bolt, he throws his arm over me, blocking me from getting out. Lord, he smells like sewage, only worse.

"Don't you even *think* about bolting, you hear me you little snot? If you so much as try anything stupid, you won't even know what hit you. You are coming to Mexico with me, you hear? Those cartel leaders will pay big money for a young wayward kid like you."

As he does this, he pulls a gun, and places it to the side of my head to show that he is serious. "*I will blow you away,*" he whispers in a sinister tone. "Now get up. You're going with me. You're lucky to be with me. I'll get you water and a sandwich. Now get a move on." He is snarling at me. Pushing the gun into my side, he walks behind me as we enter the gas station. Never taking his eyes off of me for more than a second, I wander around the gas station, paralyzed with fear, wondering where I am, and why I could be so stupid to leave home. I am faced with the very real possibility that when my family watched me leave the house in an angry frenzy, only hours after losing my mother, they may find out that I have gone missing, never to hear from or see me ever again. That thought crushes me, as dysfunctional as my family is.

Beforelong, I find myself back in the front seat of his disgusting car, where the odor has not improved. As the sun heats the windows, it makes the smell even more pungent. It is just dumbfounding to me how this guy isn't high from these fumes. Maybe he is.

We are on the road for several hours. Sometimes, he tries to make conversation with me. Other times, he sits in silence. Occasionally, he will scare me crapless with a guttural scream or cackling fit. This guy just has to be some sort of lunatic from an insane asylum. I literally could not have picked a worse car to get into for hitchhiking.

We start, stop, start, and stop, all while the gun is basically at my back the whole time.

Somewhere along the line, we stop somewhere very remote, and I can't help but think *"this would be the perfect place to kill somebody and dump the body. Nobody would even know."* I try hard to dismiss that terrifying thought out of my head, but it's hard.

The Roamer

After getting our gas and food for the night, we pull into what looks like a campsite. It's hard to tell since it's so covered in snow. He must trust that he's scared me enough that I won't run, because he gets out without even looking at me and immediately starts to shovel away a spot where he can pitch a dingy old tent he pulls from his trunk, which isn't any cleaner than the cab of his car. Within about ten minutes, something that resembles a tent is standing next to a dark group of trees, and a fire has been started. I look around, and realize that he has left his gun sitting on the picnic table. If I didn't have such an awful feeling that he is testing me, I would pick it up, shoot him, and get the hell out of here. But, my fear gets the best of me.

Now, oddly, he invites me to sit next to him on a log next to the fire.

Throughout the next two hours, he proceeds to talk to me as if he is a normal person. He asks me normal questions, and expects me to respond. After a short bit of time, I would ask him a question too. Through it all, I am terrified to ask the wrong thing for fear of setting him off and sparking an explosion.

"So really, kid, what brings you off this way? How often is it that a youngster carrying a trombone and a duffel bag is found ten miles south of St. Paul, not heading anywhere special?"

It's not like I can avoid answering him.

"My mother died a few days ago. I got into an argument with my father and I ran away."

He sits there and nods like he understands.

"It probably won't surprise you, kid, but my mother was an alcoholic, and my father was in jail for murder before I was even born," he says. "I never did have a very happy childhood."

"So is that why you're kidnapping me and taking me to Mexico?" I ask, hoping I won't set him off.

Surprisingly, he just laughs. "Mexico is gonna be great, kid. There's none of this snow, the sun shines everyday, and the drugs make you feel like you're in the purest form of meditation all the time. I've been there dozens of times since I've been your age, but this time, I got no intention of going back."

"But why do I have to go with you? I don't want to do drugs and I was hoping to start someplace new within the United States."

"I already told you, kid. Sometimes, in life, there are opportunities too good to pass up. You are one of them. Call it collateral damage, if you will. Occasionally you'll come across a great opportunity for yourself, but in the process you'll need to inconvenience or damage another person. So I'm sorry, kid, that's exactly what this is."

It doesn't seem like there's any arguing with him. Before I can defend myself, he launches into another story.

"Let me tell you about this time when I was about your age, kid. I couldn't have been older than sixteen but I know I was older than twelve. My mother, before she turned to alcohol, actually used to be a pretty good woman. At the time, she was going with this guy from California, and for a while I actually thought he was a neat guy too."

All the while he speaks, his hands shake, he impulsively pushes his scraggly hair back, and his voice goes up and down in volume. I am worried that soon, he may start screaming and decide to kill me in a fit of rage.

"There was a time that he told me he was going to take me fishing. What I didn't know is that he had talked to my mother in advance."

His face starts getting redder. I am cringing at every word he says.

"He doesn't take me to the river or any lake to go fishing. He takes me to an underground bunker which I can only describe as looking like a mad scientist's lab. I freaked out and asked him what the hell he was doing and where the fish were.

He just laughed. It was then that I found out that he had brought me there to be experimented on. My mom and her lover wanted to know what the effects of hard drugs would be on younger, skinnier guys, and they wanted to compare it to how fast it takes hold in older, bigger guys. So, kid, I'm sure you can guess what happened."

I'm still shaking with fear. "What happened?"

"My mother and her boyfriend watched as I was forced down and injected with heroin. Over the next few weeks, they watched as I slowly got hooked on the drugs. They got paid thousands of dollars to provide me as an experimental subject, and me? ME? Well. I was just exactly what you are, kid. Collateral. Damage. I got NOTHING out of that deal. Unless you count the drug addiction. I got that, I guess. But you know what, kid? I've learned to just embrace it. If I've got to be hooked on this stuff, I may as well make the best of it. That's why you're coming with me. When you and I hit Mexico, you're going to help me earn back every penny of what I was cheated out of when I was a kid. I think you are a great kid, but you're going to be collateral damage for me. Then hopefully when you get to be my age, you can find somebody to be collateral damage for you, too. You feel me there?"

His posture is firm. His voice is certain. There is no arguing with him.

"Isn't there another way? Couldn't I help you get the money for the drugs and then you let me go?"

"Sorry kid, no dice." he says as he stands up and moves toward the tent.   I've got a plan, and you're going to help me. That's that. I sure don't want to mess you up so don't go trying anything funny."

With that, he opens the tent door and motions for me to get in. If there is anything worse than sleeping all night in a tent near a man who smells like a septic tank, I don't know what it would be. Reluctantly, I move toward the tent, praying against hope that I can find some way to escape with my life.

⋀⋀⋀

The fact that it's winter and it's freezing is irrelevant to me. I spend the better part of that night choking for air, or trying my hardest to either get the courage up to leave, or come up with a better plan. Ultimately, I decide against trying to escape from the tent. He has that gun underneath his pillow and if he catches me trying to leave, I will never see the light of day ever again. I know for sure that I need to come up with a plan before we hit the border. He means it when he says that when we cross that border, there's no coming back. I decide that my best bet is going to be saying a prayer and taking a flying leap from the car, with the hope that eventually I'll be able to escape from him before he finds me. By the time he slows down and stops the car, gets out, and starts chasing me, I hope that I'll already be out of his sight. However, my timing has to be PERFECT.

When 6:00 am finally rolls around, he grunts, rolls over, rubs his eyes, and lets out a scream when he looks at me. It scares me so bad I almost make a chocolate factory out of my own pants. This guy is clearly going through drug withdrawals. That's what I think these screams and mood swings are.

"What do you want?!" I yell at him after the scream. He just stares at me and blinks harder. "Sorry," he mumbles as he starts to get moving. "I just forgot you are with me."

We pack up the tent, and, keeping his eyes on me all the while, we get back into the rotting car. The smell makes my eyes bleed and burn. At least, that's what it feels like. This slime ball has another thing coming later today, and I sure hope my last memories on earth are not of him chasing me with a gun, screaming something about "collateral damage."

We are on the road again, and we pass a sign that says "Welcome to Iowa." I figure I should do this soon, before I am so far from

54

Minnesota that it will take years to get back. But, that's just it. I'm not sure I want to be back. I want to be away from this creep, that's for sure. But is being with him making me wish I was back with my alcoholic father? I can't say it is. But, I don't have time to think on it for long.

Soon, we come to a sign that says a town is only five miles away. This is my cue – since soon we will be approaching a part of the road where the speed limit is on the slower end. We are going fast enough to where he will have to go a ways in order to come to a complete stop, but slow enough to where I won't die if I jump out (hopefully).

I have everything with me in the front seat. Looking over at the man, I don't see any signs that he thinks anything is about to happen. I look at the door. It's unlocked, and

I can make the jump. The side of the road has a ton of snow - which I hope will provide a nice buffer to the fall I'm about to take.

Saying a prayer, and grabbing all of my belongings, I throw the door handle, and jump out of the car in a massive leap of faith. From here, everything happens in slow motion. I hear his scream, the squeal of the brakes, and a huge bang.

Suddenly, the slow motion stops and I hit the ground like a big rock. This fast, I feel like my brain is shaking around the inside of my skull. I tumble, and roll over and over and over again, I feel like it's never going to end. When I finally come to a stop, I lay there for a second staring up at the sky, not able to hear anything. Then everything goes dark.

⋯⋀⋀⋀⋯

When I wake up next, I am freezing in the snow. It is almost dark, and I hear a tremendous ringing inside of my head. I instantly become aware of a tremendous pain in my right arm, which seems to be pinned behind my back.

Somehow, I manage to sit up, but not without awful pain shooting up my arm and into my brain. I don't know how long I scream after that. Once I am able to get my vision clear, I look around me. Terrified that I am only a second away from being re-captured by the freak that picked me up, I am hyper aware and edgy as a squirrel cornered by a dog.

Miraculously, I don't see him at all. The area is barren. No cars, no people, no animals, not even a noise. It's eerily quiet now that my ears have somewhat stopped ringing. It's not easy to see right now, but I can still make out the horizon line. There is nothing that even resembles a building or a town anywhere in sight. The only thing I can see is a small spattering of blood in the snow from my jump out of the car. My arm is killing me more each second, so I decide to collapse. The position of the sun tells me that the night is just beginning. I am still terrified that the crazy man who picked me up is going to find me again, so I decide I should hunker down for the night, and pick up again in the morning. Although, I think I have gained a healthy fear of hitchhiking now. In fact, I don't know if I ever want to ride in the passenger seat again for as long as I live.

The Roamer

As the night wears on, the cold wind bites at every inch of my exposed skin. I have terrible road rash all over my legs and arms in addition to my injured arm, which I can't use to squeeze myself to contain warmth. Through it all, I can't stop thinking about Mom. What she would think if she could know what I am going through right now. How she would absolutely wallop the guy who dared try to take me to Mexico. It occurs to me that I miss my mom - I may not miss Dad, but I sure do miss my mom. I feel myself welling up to cry, but I suppress it. Raynold Penfield does not cry. I'm too tough for stuff like that. Instead, I just lay here - thinking about where Mom may be and what she is seeing right now. It is such a stupid and unfair world - where good people like Mom die young, and jerks like the guy who took me, still roam free.

Chapter Four

I awake in the morning, after not getting nearly enough sleep. When the cold wasn't keeping me awake, the pain from my arm certainly was. Soon enough, the last of the adrenaline had worn off, and I felt every single bit of pain from my injury. On more than one occasion, I nearly throw up just from the pain. Nevertheless, I did manage to get some sleep.

Sitting up, squinting in the early morning bright sun, I wonder why the sun can shine so bright and it can still be this damn cold. I try to think of what my next steps are to be. Deciding I will walk and think at the same time, I cautiously manage to get up and start moving down the road in the direction the crazy man had been taking me down. Suddenly, with a fair bit of shock, I notice what had caused the loud squealing and banging noise that I had heard the second before I blacked out.

I can only theorize what caused this. What I see is so disturbing, I doubt I'll ever be able to erase it from my mind. I see the car, nearly split entirely in two, crashed into a tree near a culvert. There is a large patch of ice in the middle of the road. The crazy man who kidnapped me is hanging out the driver's side window - or, at least most of him is. Something tells me that he won't be making it the rest of the way to Mexico. What I think happened is, judging by the tire tracks burned into the ice, he saw me escape, slammed on the brakes, turned around to shoot me, and lost control of the vehicle, causing the big crash into the tree. The injury to my arm was probably when I landed on it behind my back. Not broken, but close. Not nearly as bad as it could have been.

I'm in the middle of nowhere near the Iowa border. It's freezing, I'm injured, and I'm scared. I feel so far from home I don't know how I'll ever get back. The loneliness my heart feels is now worse than the injury to my arm; and it's starting to become unbearable. Yet still, it's hard to wish myself back home with my dad.

Moving past the car and onward down the road, I keep moving on - dragging what's left of my bag that survived the fall along with me.   Unfortunately, my trombone is not among them. The fall from the car damaged it so badly, there is no hope I'll ever play it again. The thought comes to me that it's good the trombone was damaged - it's so much easier not having to carry it, and it was a dumb idea to bring it along with me in the first place.

The only hope I have now is that somebody sane will pick me up, or I can make it to the next town before I collapse from exhaustion and thirst. At the moment, I am not very willing to bet on either.

I don't know for how long I walk, but I slowly observe the sun moving from my left side, across the horizon line, and on toward the right side. The few cars that pass me walking don't stop, as if they are purposefully avoiding me. Right as I am about to give up hope and surrender to my fate as a roamer, the sun begins to go down and I am surprised yet again.

Pulling up leisurely alongside me looks to be a minivan towing some sort of travel trailer. Truly, this is an unusual sight, as it's the middle of winter in the Midwest. But also, I stand astonished – because I have never seen a real one in my entire life - only pictures. I stand there staring at it as they drive past me. I briefly glimpse what looks like three or four people looking at me from the van as they drive by. They don't make it too far ahead of me before I hear the van screech to a stop, followed by a man and a woman getting out of the van.

"Everything okay?" the man asks. "You look like you've been through the meat grinder, young man!"

Truly, I have yet to take a look at the full extent of my injuries, but his remark didn't surprise me given the fact that I had literally just jumped from a moving car. My face probably looks like a wreck.

"Yeah," I mutter, not sure I want to accept their help after all. Part of me now wants to tough it out and make it all on my own, just so I can selfishly rub it in my dad's face later on.

"Are you sure?" asks the woman. "Your face looks rough, young man. Did you get into a fight or a car accident?"

Not sure what to tell them without spilling my guts, I start with a half truth. "There was an incident with a car..." I start. But before I even finish, their arms are around me leading me toward their travel trailer. "Well, come on. You can tell us the rest later. Let us help you get these wounds cleaned up. You are probably cold, thirsty, and starving!"

They had me there. I am soon led up the steps and into their travel trailer. I have never seen anything so incredible. It's like a full on mini house that you can actually tow behind your car. I decide right here and now that no matter what, I NEED to have one of these for myself one day. My family will love it.

Soon enough, a young boy comes up the stairs of the trailer looking for what I can assume are his parents. "Hey, are we going again soon? I'm cold!" he asks, before making eye contact with me for the first time. He looks at me like I'm something out of a bizarre action movie, as if he's not sure what to think I am. I certainly don't know what to say to him, since I stand out like I'm a dead rat in a punch bowl. So, I just nod my head. "Soon, Matthew. Soon. We need to take care of this young man first!" He heads back toward the van right then.

Beforelong, there is a turkey and cheese sandwich and a glass of water in front of me, and I don't think I've been so thankful for anything in my entire life. I think I would have inhaled all of it all at once, but I was forced to eat slower, as the woman was checking the injuries to my arm and face.

"Goodness sakes," she says with concern in her voice. "Tell me again, how did this happen?" She is patting the open wounds and cleaning them with some solution that stings like hell, but seems to be working.

There's really no two ways around it now. These guys clearly aren't anything like the guy who tried to kidnap me, and they must be pretty well-to-do if they can afford a nice trailer like this one. So, I decide to tell them a condensed version of my story. I start with how my mom passed away, I got into a fight with my dad, I was hitchhiking hoping to go somewhere to start over, and I ended up with a bad guy who threatened to kill me, so I jumped out, and ended up killing himself against a tree. That's when they managed to find me.

"Oh my goodness," the woman says, taking a deep breath. "Well, maybe you should stay with us for a few days, uh - uh..." she pauses as if she is trying to remember something. "What's your name, son? I don't know if we ever even shared our names!"

"Raynold," I say, "Raynold Penfield. You?"

"I'm Julie, this is my husband Wayne, and our son Matthew is in the van. We are on our way down to The Ozarks. We love the National Forest down that way, and Matthew has never been there. He's so excited to get away from the snow for a while. Why don't you come with us and recover for a bit?"

I am hesitant. It sounds so enticing, but I just finished a spell where I was kidnapped and told I was going to be collateral damage for a drug cartel in Mexico. I'm not sure I want to immediately trust this family that seems too good to be true.

"I'm not sure," I say truthfully, but I shade the reason

why. "I don't have any money, and I don't really want to impose on your vacation."

To that, Julie just laughs. "Don't you worry about that, son. If Wayne makes enough money to buy a travel trailer like this one, he makes enough to support one additional passenger. You seem like a fine young man. Please join us!"

They seem genuine enough, and admittedly, I felt skeptical of the first guy before I even got into the car, and got in anyway. I have a terrible feeling I would regret turning them down later, so I say "okay." I would be turning away a massive opportunity to move faster, and doing it a lot safer.

"Fantastic!" Julie exclaims as she finishes wrapping up my arm. "Wayne will get your things to the trunk. You can sit next to Matthew in the back seat. There's plenty of room. Let's go!"

Leaving the trailer, I make my way toward the minivan pulling the trailer. Matthew eyes me with caution as I move in next to him. Clearly, I look like a roamer, and it's plain to anyone that he looks apprehensive about me sitting next to him as they head south on vacation.

"Don't worry, I won't bother you," I whisper. He doesn't answer, he just looks toward his parents as they pull onto the road again. So begins the next leg of my big adventure.

Chapter Five

We are on the road for what feels like a really long time. Hours turn into days, stopping periodically, getting on the road again. Over the next few days, there are times when they try to engage me in conversation and there are times when the music plays and we all just sit in silence watching the world go by. It is then that I notice the snow starts to fade further and further away as we head further south into what I can imagine is Missouri or Arkansas. Iowa disappears faster than grains of sand slip through your fingers.

During the times when we all chat together, I learn that their last name is Morrison, and they are also from Minnesota. They love to travel in their trailer, and have been all across the country, from California, to Maine. However, their favorite spot to visit is the place they are heading to right now - the Ozark Mountains. I have never been there myself, but I have seen pictures on postcards and the closer we get, the more excited I become.

It's a weird feeling, honestly. This family is so kind and so welcoming. They haven't thought twice about the fact that I don't have any money on me. They found me on the side of the road and they took me in as their own. Even

Matthew is starting to talk to me and open up a bit more after starting off really shy. This is all a welcome change from my first chauffeur.

I dig in my backpack during one of the long stretches of driving. We are almost there but there's still a good chunk of time left. Just enough time to write out this journey so far on the paper I brought in my bag. Matthew is busy reading, Julie is sleeping, and Wayne is driving. It's a perfect opportunity to write – even though it's something I usually hate to do. But since a teacher isn't making me do it this time, I don't mind it at all.

Day One: The Morrisons picked me up off of the side of the road looking dirty, damaged, and depressed. They load me up into their vehicle, along with what little belongings I have, and continue on their way. I tell them about my mother, my fight with my father, running away from home, my kidnapping, and the car incident. We don't drive long before we pull over for the night – and I spend my first true comfortable night since before Mom died. I was so relieved that night, I felt myself wanting to cry, but I still didn't. I slept better that night than I had in over a week.

Day Two: We get up at the break of dawn and have cereal and toast for breakfast. During breakfast, they tell us that we have two more full days of driving before we get to the part of the mountains where we will be staying. After breakfast and getting the trailer ready, we start driving south – mostly through Kansas City. Around this time is when I have my first real conversation with Matthew. He's younger than me, and for the most part on the quieter side, but he's a good kid. Much better than my old friends Greg and Gordy, anyhow. I'm amazed, because considering how different he is than the two of them, I like Matthew way better. He's eleven, and I'm fourteen, but you'd never guess he's younger than me by that much. He's way more mature than anybody I palled around with back in St. Paul, which is saying a lot. We talked movies, old war stories, what games we liked to play, and told stories about our families and friends. Every once in a while, his mom would smile back at us, then return to her book or nap. I lost track of the number of times we laughed, and for a while, I even forgot I had a hurt arm and was still recovering from road rash. Once we made it to our last rest stop before our final destination, we cooked hotdogs over the campfire, and enjoyed the fact that there was hardly *any snow to be seen anywhere. It's really starting to warm up. I enjoyed my second night in a real bed, and my excitement is building for seeing those Ozarks.*

Day Three: This way and that way, we travel onward toward the Ozarks. The more time that passes, the more I feel like this is my family, and is where I'm meant to be.   I figure it won't be long, though, before I have to answer a bunch more questions about my real family, why I'm here, and what my plans are.   I'm not looking forward to that, but so far they haven't said anything so I'm enjoying all this while I can.   Looks like we are about to pull into the campsite right now.   Can't wait!"

"Well, here we are!" Julie jubilantly exclaims as we exit the vehicle and start to look around. "We'll be here for the next two weeks. I know it doesn't look like much yet, but once we go hiking and get a good view of those mountains, you'll be awestruck!"

I watch as Wayne starts to get the trailer all set up to live in for the next two weeks. What intrigues me most is when he starts to plug things into wooden sticks coming out of the ground.

"What are you doing?" I ask him, truly intrigued. He turns around and smiles at me as he says "these are our hookups, Raynold! What I'm plugging in right now is our electricity, so whenever you turn on the lights in the camper, they'll work. I just finished hooking up the water, so whenever you want to take a shower or wash your hands, you've got water to do it. And after I finish here, I'll hook up the septic line, so whenever you flush the toilet, well...you get the idea. Pretty amazing what these things can do, huh?" he asks me.

I am too amazed to even answer him. This is so far beyond anything I ever could have imagined. Why doesn't anybody just live like this all the time?

Throughout the rest of the afternoon, Matthew and I help get the rest of the luggage from the vehicle into the camper. It's during this time that he decides to ask me about my family, and how I ended up with them.

"So, how did you end up with an arm injury like that on the side of the road again? I know you already told my parents, but I don't remember," says Matthew, immediately gaining a look on his face that shows that he regrets being so bold. But, I don't care. They have been nothing but kind to me, and I trust them.

"I lost my mother a few weeks ago," I say slowly and sullenly. "Then I got into a bad fight with my father. It ended with me storming out and hitchhiking out of St. Paul. I got into a car with somebody I shouldn't have. He was planning on taking me to Mexico to be sold into the drug trade. As we were leaving one morning, I jumped out of the car, and I landed on my arm after. Then he lost control of the car and crashed into a tree. I started walking down the road, not knowing where I would end up next, and that's when your family found me."

He stares at me as if he truly can't believe what he is hearing. "No freaking way," he says. "You could write a great adventure book about this!" he says with a smile spreading across his face. I smile too, but I say "thanks, but I don't read. Plus, my story isn't exactly over yet. I won't be with you guys forever."

The smile starts to fade from his face. Changing the subject, he says "I'm sorry to hear about your mom, and your dad too. I can't imagine life without my mom, and even though my dad can be fussy once in a while, he's still a great dad."

I can't help but be a little jealous. "That's awesome," I say. Right then is when we have hauled the last of the luggage into the camper.

"Well. What's next?!" he asks me. "What do you want to go do?" I can't believe he is asking ME this. "I don't know, don't your parents have plans?"

He fidgets with the zipper on his jacket. "Not today," he says. "They're exhausted from the drive here. What do you say we walk down to the gift shop and raid the candy counter?"

I feel myself getting embarrassed again. "I don't have any money," I say without much confidence. Reaching into his pockets, he pulls out several dollar bills and coins. Smiling at me, he says "let's go!"

Trying not to let myself get upset that I can't take care of myself, I walk along with Matthew. On the walk, he starts singing the US Air Force Fight Song. I haven't heard it for a long time, but I still remember the words, all of them! I've never been much of a singer, but I join in anyway.

"Off we go! Into the wild blue yonder, climbing high into the sun! Here they come, zooming to meet our thunder,

*At 'em boys! Give 'em your gun! Give
'em your gun!*
*Down we dive, spouting our flame
from under, off with one hell of a roar!
We live in fame, or go down in flame!
Nothing'll stop the US Air Force!"*

By the end of it, we are both
laughing our butts off, and for a
while, I forget the reason I'm even
on this trip. I feel right at home
with these guys.

Walking into the gift shop, I
start laughing as I get an idea. The
last thing I want to do is get
Matthew into trouble, but at the
same time, I am just aching for a bit
of mischief. He seems like the kind
of kid who wouldn't start any
trouble himself, but may follow
along if someone else leads.

"Hey," I say. "There are a
bunch of stink bombs for sale on the
shelf over there. What if we let one

off and toss it behind the counter when the cashier isn't looking?" As I say it, I laugh even harder. The thought alone is hilarious. Last school year, Greg, Gordy and I had let one off during the middle of a math test. We got in huge trouble for it, but it was so worth getting out of the test.

He looks hesitant. "What do we do after we let it off?" he asks, clearly unsure. I just laugh again. "Then, we RUN!" I make a motion for the door. "The cashier won't know what hit her!"

Slowly but surely, a smile creeps across Matthew's face. "Okay. But I don't want to get into trouble! My parents won't be happy if we get kicked out of here."

"Don't worry," I say, I'm an expert at not getting caught. Just stick tight to me, and you'll be fine."

Stink bomb in hand, we walk around the store trying to look as if we are going to buy something. The cashier has her nose buried in a book. Slowly and as sneaky as I possibly can, I activate the stink bomb and toss it behind the counter and start to move quickly toward the door. When it pops, we see the cashier look back, but immediately go back to her book. Just outside the door ten seconds later, we hear her start to wail.

"AHHHHHHHH!"

Matthew and I are cackling with laughter from the bushes around the corner. Peeking in the window, we see her with her hands over her nose and mouth, running all over the place looking for the stink bomb. It's the most hilarious thing I've caused since I put plastic wrap over the top of my dad's toilet. We stay there laughing for a good minute, and only crouch down when she comes out the door wailing.

"WHO IS THE MENACE RESPONSIBLE FOR THIS?! I'LL GET YOU, I SWEAR I WILL!"

She looks around but she doesn't spot us. She goes back inside, and even from here we can hear her freaking out over the smell. Once more, we break into a laughing fit, and only stop when we need to catch our breath.

"That is the funniest thing I've ever seen!" Matthew chortles. "And what's better, that lady didn't even look up from her book even once, so I bet she didn't even see who we were!"

"Not a chance!" I say, impressed that he is going along with this. "Hey, sorry we didn't get to raid the candy counter though."

"This was WAY better than raiding the candy counter, are you kidding me!" Matthew says. "That was the most fun I've had in ages!"

We get up slowly and start to walk back. "It's too bad you didn't grab more than one," Matthew says. "We could play some GREAT pranks on my parents with these!"

I was going to surprise him, but I figure now may be a better time. Smiling, I empty my pockets and show him what's inside. Grinning, he stares in awe at what I have to show him. What he didn't know is that I grabbed every stink bomb in the box, and put them into my pocket. The one we set off behind the counter was only one of three. I was thinking that I would save the other two for a rainy day.

"That's awesome!" he says, the grin never fading from his face. My parents won't know what hit them!"

"We should be nice to your parents," I say. "They've been great so far."

"Yeah," he says. "Maybe we should set it off outside and make them think it's a skunk, instead of doing it in the camper itself. They may laugh more then!"

"True!" I say, right as we make it back to the camper. We are just in time for dinner. Wayne is making a campfire, and Julie is preparing the hotdogs. We spend the rest of the evening chatting and laughing the night away. These guys truly feel like my real family.

Shortly before bed, after changing the dressing on my arm, Julie asks the question I've been dreading.

"What's to happen regarding the situation with your father, Raynold? Have you contacted him at all since you left?"

I feel myself start to tense up inside as I think about what may be on his mind right now. I really damaged any hope of a relationship with him by doing this. Flashbacks begin to hit me - me striking him, him shoving me into the corner, the busted bottle of booze...

"Raynold? Are you alright?" Julie asks. Coming back, I nod at her. "I'm not sure what my dad is up to. I can imagine he's busy with working, with my younger brother, and probably planning my mother's funeral."

Julie's face turns to some combination of sympathy and concern. She clearly doesn't feel right about me being with them while my family doesn't know where I am and is dealing with a lot of trouble.

"Raynold, I think it's best that you call your father to let him know

where you are and what you are up
to. God forbid, if Matthew were in
this situation, I know Wayne and I
would appreciate that, at the very
least. Please know you are welcome
to be with us, but even if you are
having trouble with your family,
you should let them know that you
are safe and are thinking about
them."

Truthfully, I haven't been
thinking about them almost at all,
as shameful as it is to admit it. Deep
down, I know Julie has a point, so I
make a promise to her right then.
"I'll call my father soon. I promise.
I'll let him know where we are and
that I'm okay."

Julie smiles right then.
"That's good. You have a great
night. I hope you have been
enjoying your time with us so far.
We just love having you with us.
Matthew thinks the world of you."

"He's a really good guy," I say. I'm not much of a sappy person, but it's true. Matthew is probably the greatest guy I've ever known and I haven't even known him that long. Worlds better than Greg or Gordy ever were.

"Sleep good," she says as she walks toward her bedroom. That night, echoes of my father's booming voice ripple through my mind. I try to ignore them, but when I close my eyes and try to tune it out, I can see my mother's sad, hollow face...wanting me to be a better person. What would she think if she knew I had hit my father, ditched home, and hitchhiked my way to the Ozarks, only to find out that I love this family more than the one I was being raised in? It was enough to keep me awake thinking for almost the entire night.

The Roamer

᭶ᖰ

Throughout the rest of that week, I hang with the family. I punt calling my father as long as I possibly can. The last voice I want to hear right now is his.

We have so many fun adventures in the Ozarks, honestly I begin to lose count of them all! We start by hiking - there are lots of trails around here. During this time, we talk about everything from sports, to cars, to food, and even books. They don't make anything sound boring. Better yet - they don't yell at Matthew. They don't talk down to him or correct him constantly or make him feel stupid. It's something that's new to me.

We also found a swimming hole that had cliffs so high we could jump right off of them and into the water! I was scared nearly out of my shorts at first - but I did it. It astonished me that it is still winter in St. Paul. But the second I hit the water, it was incredibly cold, I knew without a doubt that it's still winter!

I discover quickly enough that I do NOT like s'mores - they are so sweet, I swear I can feel the sugar on my teeth and in my bloodstream for days after. No candy I've ever had would ever be sweeter than s'mores!

The park we are parked at is absolutely gorgeous. It's hard to beat the view from the mountain top - which we hiked to more than once! It's a steep walk, and each time we get to the top, I'm about dying for breath. When I was living back home, every once in a while I would sneak a cigarette from my father. It sure helped me relax, but I'm starting to think that if I hadn't smoked those cigarettes, I wouldn't have such a hard time walking up to the top of the mountain!

But nothing - and I mean, nothing - can compare to the feeling when we are walking through what I consider the crowned jewel of our trip so far: St. Francis National Forest.

When I stand underneath all of those tall trees, I feel as though the world has swallowed me whole. Looking all around me, I see nothing but tall tree trunks sweeping the area. The trees go for miles around and seem like they can reach Heaven. I find myself wishing I wish I could climb one of them so I could say hi to my mom. The trees are an absolute wonder - and I want more than anything to come here again - in a camper trailer of my own.

During the times we weren't hiking, or swimming, or exploring, we were trying new places to eat, checking out arcades, sleeping in, chatting over a campfire, or roaming the woods in search of bugs and snakes.

At the end of the most amazing week, Matthew and I are sitting around the campfire one morning. Wayne has just started it so he could cook some pancakes for breakfast. I had just rolled out of bed and so had Matthew.

"I hate to ask this, but how much longer do you think you'll be staying with us?" he asks me with an unsure look in his eyes.

I shrug my shoulders. "Don't know. I wish I could stay forever. This has been the best week of my life when I thought for sure it would be the worst."

I sit down on the ground near the fire. "I just wish I had an idea in mind of where I am going to go next, you know? I guess all I had in mind when I left my house is that I wanted to be away from my father, and I was mad at him about my mom dying. But now that reality has set in again, I don't know what's next. You guys have spoiled me big time, but I doubt I can stay with you forever. You guys are going home in a matter of days. I can't go with you then."

"Sure you can!" Matthew says. "I've always wanted a brother! You and I can go to school where I go to school! We can ride bikes, mess with the teachers, build a fort in the woods behind my house, we can..."

Matthew drones on about all the things he wants us to do, but I quickly become aware of something far more concerning. My rear end starts to quickly feel like it's on fire!

Standing up quickly and glancing down my backside,

Matthew's thoughts are interrupted by my scream - almost as high as a little girl's. My entire butt and back of my legs are *covered* in fire ants. I look down, only to realize there is a swarm of them. I had just sat down on the ant hill of a colony of fire ants.

Jumping up and down and running all over the campsite, I soon attract the attention of Wayne and Julie, and I'm sure plenty of animals in the woods. I am brushing, running, smacking, rubbing, burning, screaming, yelling...you name it. I have never felt a burning pain like this ever before in my entire life!

Finally, the ants look like they are gone and I run inside the camper with fire coming out of my eyes and a wide open mouth.

Julie is close behind and she quickly begins assessing the

damage. Beforelong, I have a backside full of cream, and my legs are all bandaged up, along with my arm, which is still wrapped up good.

When I've finally caught my breath, Julie asks if I am okay. "I think so," I say, breathing heavily. We then walk outside to the front of the camper where Wayne and Matthew await us. Then, without warning, all of us start to laugh hysterically, especially Matthew.

"You should have SEEN the look on your face when you first realized those ants were crawling up your leg!" he says through guffaws.

"Let's consider that KARMA for the little stink bomb that you and Matthew planted outside the camper the other day!" says Wayne. If you thought I wouldn't find this, you were sadly mistaken!" He holds up the spent stink bomb in his hand. "Now I don't have to worry about putting hot sauce on you boys' next hotdog!" Wayne laughs.

"I just about had a heart attack when I heard Raynold screaming!" Julie adds. "I thought he was getting mauled by a BEAR!"

"Truly, I think I'd rather be mauled by a bear than go through that again!" I say, still laughing.

Soon enough, Wayne and Julie return to what they were doing, and Matthew and I resume chatting.

"You know, Matthew, I've been thinking. This has been fun and all, but I don't think we can continue this forever. Before long, I'm going to have to face up to my own reality. Soon, this vacation will be over for you guys, and then what happens with me? I'll have to go on my own way again, somehow. There isn't much time left in this trip for you guys. You may as well enjoy it while it's here."

"That's crazy, Ray! We love having you here with us and we want you to finish it out! After we get back from here, you could stay with us! Like I was saying, we could go to school together, I could introduce you to my friends, we could..."

"It's a nice thought, Matthew, but really, how realistic is that? Do your parents seriously want me hanging around with them forever after meeting me for the first time around a week ago? I really don't think so."

He tries to talk again, but I don't want to talk about it anymore. Though I'd never admit it to anyone, I am afraid of crying. I have loved my time with this family, and it's taught me more about what kind of things I want for my family later on. But I can't stay with them forever. I'll forever be thankful to them for taking care of me when I needed it. But, now I'm well enough to where I can continue on. It's time for me to say goodbye and be on my own once again.

I walk into the camper toward my bed and my limited amount of belongings. I start to gather them, thinking I'll maybe leave a written message for Wayne, Julie, and Matthew.

Right as I am thinking that's what I'll do, Wayne comes into the camper with something in his hands. "Surprise!" he says, handing it to me. I can't believe it – it's my trombone case! Looking inside, I see the trombone looking almost as good as new.

"What? How?!" I ask, confused how he even got this.

"I picked it up about 50 feet from where we found you when we picked you up. I polished it up and pounded out a few of the dents, and voila! Looks pretty good, doesn't it? Let's hear you play it!"

Suddenly shy, I close the case again, not wanting to embarrass myself. It would do no good to let him know that I don't pay any attention in my trombone lessons. Fortunately, I have an excuse.

"My arm still isn't feeling up to it," I say, "but thank you for fixing it."

"Well, if your arm isn't up to this, then why does it look like you're about to walk out the door and leave us?" he asks without warning. He's pretty perceptive.

"I appreciate all you guys have done for me, but I can't stay here forever. I need to keep going on my way."

By now, Julie and Matthew have entered the camper.

"You are thinking of LEAVING?" Julie asks, stunned. "Reynold, you are in no shape to travel alone! Please, for heaven's sake, stay with us until we head back home! You can stay with us for a while until things with your family get settled."

"The truth is, I don't know if I'm going back to my family. I intend on doing what you asked me and calling my father to let him know I'm okay. But as of now, I have no intention of going back there. I want to start over. I have had fun with you guys and I know already that I want to come back to this place. But I can't let myself be a burden to you. I'll be sure to reach out again once I'm settled and you can come visit me."

It goes on like this for quite a while. They aren't taking it well, and they beg me to stay. Matthew especially. I swear I can see the glimmer of tears in his eyes. I thank them sincerely for all they did for me, including nursing me back to health after I jumped from a moving car.

"This isn't the end for us," I say. "I'll definitely be back!" I say this as I start to walk away from the campsite after giving hugs with lots of tears in between. The last I see of them for the time being is of them standing together watching me walk down the road toward the exit of the park. I shout one last thing before they get out of earshot - "I promise - I'll call my dad!" And with that, the Morrisons are gone. My heart aches at the pain I've caused them, but it's reassuring to know that I will see them again.

Chapter Six

The first thing I do once I reach the exit of the park is find a phone. After taking a deep breath, using the coins Julie left me with, I dial the number to my house. The operator connects me, and I wait for the monotonous ringing to pass.

"Hello?" a voice grumbles on the other end. It's my dad.

"Hi, Dad," I say without much enthusiasm. There is a pause, but I can almost sense that he's trying to figure out if it's actually me.

"Ray, is that you?" he asks me as smoothly as I've ever heard him talk. "I didn't think we'd ever hear from you again. None of us did. Where the devil are you? And when will you be home? Your sisters and brother are worried sick."

I notice that he didn't say that *he* is worried sick. I don't know if I am ready to spill everything over to him, especially with the way he behaved just shortly before I left!

"I'm not telling anybody anything about where I am! In fact, I'm just following through on a promise I made. I didn't actually want to call you, I just was trying to-"

"Ray!" Dad shouts. "I'm in no mood to discuss our last interaction. You have no idea how much trouble we are in back home. When your mother died, all the bills eventually caught up to us and are coming due rather quickly."

He pauses. I wait to see if he continues. This could be a real moment of vulnerability for him.

"I – I – I need your help, Ray. It's been hell without you here. We are at risk of losing the house, and I am facing a very real danger of losing Keith to the state."

Okay, THAT I wasn't expecting. But, there it is. His plea for me to come back.

"Why should I come back to help you after what you did and said to me? What makes you think you deserve my help?"

"Can you not make this about you for one second?!" Dad shouts. I let him yell, but I stay silent. Both he and I know that I'm the one with leverage here.

Finally, he sighs. "I shouldn't have done what I did on that day. I'm sorry. Neither of us made the right decisions in that moment, and that includes me. Things will be different in my behavior if you come home. Please."

Now, it's happening. I have Dad right where I thought he would never be. Sounding vulnerable, begging for help, regretting what he did. I could live in this moment and really milk it for all it's worth. Part of me so badly wants to do so. I want him to feel the way I've felt. But...I don't.

"I don't know how fast I can get home, Dad. I'm so far from St. Paul right now."

"Just try," he says. "We need you. Let me know when you're close and I'll help however I can."

All of it starts to hit me – everything I've been suppressing since Mom died. "Okay. I'll come home."

"Thank you," Dad says. Then the phone goes dead. The ringing of the dial tone echoes in my mind.

Chapter Seven

Walking out of the phone booth, carrying everything I have, I realize I left my trombone behind. I'm too far ahead now to care, though, and now I have too much on my mind. I have worked so hard to suppress all my sadness about my mother's death, that I honestly am not prepared now that it's bubbling to the surface again.

I begin my journey north. This time, I am going to be wise of the company I keep. I find it hard to believe that I'll find anybody as great as the Morrisons, but hopefully I won't be kidnapped by anymore vagabonds.

As I walk, I think of all of the fun I had with Matthew. The look on the woman's face when the stink bomb went off. The jumping up and down when the ants attacked my backside. The late night talks. The laughs. The family. The security I felt...

As I walk along the highway, I see the stars. They sparkle like glitter amongst the clear, endless sky. I think to myself: "I wonder if my mom is up there, watching me head home to help my family."

I am lost in this daydream, when I hear a rustling noise from some bushes behind me. Turning around, thinking I will see a cat or some other animal, I see a flash of black, when all of a sudden, I feel a blunt heaviness on my head, and everything goes dark in an instant.

‧‧‧

Where am I? As I start to regain consciousness, I become keenly aware that something awful has happened. Whatever it is, I have a feeling I would rather be in that creep's car again than here.

Suddenly, I am stunned when a liquid is thrown into my face, and my eyes instantly begin to burn.

"AHHHHHHHHH!" I scream, as I rub my eyes, which only proceeds to make it worse. "What the hell is that?!"

I hear chortling, but I can't see any of them. Whatever they just threw on me is starting to really burn my skin as well as my eyes.

Finally, the pain subsides enough to where I can make out the shapes and faces of the person or people who are laughing at me. There are four people in front of me that I have never once seen before.

"What. Do. You. Want?" I manage to get out. My eyes still burn and my vision is hazy.

They look at each other. "Don't believe him. He knows why he's here."

"Damn right he does," another one says.

"But, since he's playing stupid, let's entertain him," the one in the center says.

I can't believe what I'm about to hear. I've never seen these guys before in my LIFE.

"You're part of the gang that stole money off our kingpin. You know something, or you have the money.   Better either fess up or cough up!"

My jaw is on the floor, or at least it feels like it. How - literally how - do these guys think I'm part of a gang?   Do I give off gangster vibes?   Did I look as if I have something hidden as I walked down the highway?

I don't have time to think of why, before one of them hits me across the face. I feel the hot swipe of pain.

"Tell   us!   Where's   the money?!"

"I don't know what you're talking about!   I don't have any money! I'm just trying to get home to my family!"

"Bull,"   says   the   big   guy. "Search him!" he adds.

As if I haven't been humiliated enough, they proceed to search every inch of my belongings, and body...for money. Then, things start to get worse.

As my vision slowly returns to normal, I find myself looking around what looks to be some warehouse. Only, I get the feeling I'm not anywhere near where I was when they picked me up.

They bring me to a table, and lay me flat, tying my arms down. Never have I been more terrified and humiliated in my entire life.

Before I know it, another round of painful, burning liquid is thrown into my face. My scream never leaves me, it hurts so bad. The pain is white-hot, like lightning. It explodes in your brain and is utterly relentless. Whatever this is, it's powerful stuff.

"TALK!" screams one of the men, as they all stand over me.

I'm too busy shouting over how bad my eyes hurt, and not

being able to do anything to them, which may be just as well. If I rub whatever this is into my eyes, I may well never see normally ever again.

"I. Don't. Know. What. You. Are. Talking. About!" I say as forcefully as I can, yet I still sound weak.

Throughout the next torturous hour, each of the men take turns screaming at me about money, taking turns whipping me and threatening me with more liquid. I finally learned what it is - vinegar, with the juices of some of the hottest peppers in the world squeezed into it. No wonder my eyes feel like they are on absolute fire and my skin feels like it wants to fall off.

Finally, they give up. They realize that I'm not about to give them any information and they've torn all my belongings apart. They must realize that I'm innocent. The problem now becomes...what are they going to do with me?

"Alright, twerp," says one of the men. "Time for some fun. You don't want to give us the info we need? Fine. But I don't think you'll be getting out of this place alive."

"Are you going to kill me?" I ask, defeatedly.

"Oh, no," says the big guy. "We are going to have way more fun than that. Just you wait."

The four of them cackle with laughter.

"You'll be happy to know, kid - we are going to let you go..."

I start to breathe a sigh of relief, but it's short lived. No way they are letting me off this easy. There's a catch, I just know it.

"Maybe we should tell you our names. Don't worry, they aren't our real names, so don't go thinking you can incriminate us," the big guy says.

The other guys laugh. "Who the hell are you kidding, John?!" he says, turning to me. With an evil look in his eyes, he adds "he couldn't get out of this place if he *tried.*"

Smiling, John continues. "Well, as you already know, I'm John. This is Jeff, Joe, and Bill, he says, pointing to each of the evil men.

"Now, what's your name?" Joe asks me.

Sneering at them, I look away instead of answering. Joe doesn't take too kindly to that.

Running up to me with more spicy vinegar, he threatens to throw more in my face. I will do literally anything to avoid having that stuff thrown at me again.

"Raynold!" I shout. "But, just call me Ray."

Truly, I don't care what they call me, just as long as they let me go.

"Well Ray, we thought for sure you had our kingpin's money, but on second thought, you are *way* too smart for us. In fact, you are so smart, we have some challenges for you.

The others start to snicker, obviously knowing what is coming. I am absolutely dreading whatever it is.

"We have some challenges for you, *Ray*. We'll make you a deal."

All four of them are staring down at me pitifully, yet also with a sinister look, as if they have no hope for me, and they couldn't care less.

"You are in our headquarters, Ray. Out in the middle of the woods, far from most roads, easy place to avoid detection by cops. So don't get any ideas."

Attention shifts to Bill, who describes in detail what I am about to do.

"Just down that hallway there, there are three locked rooms. Each room has – shall we say – a *surprise* inside. Your job is to either stay alive a certain amount of time inside, a time only we know. Or, beat whatever is inside. If you come out alive, then you are free to go! If you don't...well, then, better luck next time."

The men cackle with a chorus of evil laughter.

"Or, you know...you could just pay up the money and we'll let you go without any of this."

Defeated, my thoughts drift to my father, who wouldn't be able to help me out of this. The whole reason I'm coming back is because my family doesn't have any money after my mother's cancer. But I don't expect these demonic gremlins to understand that.

Before I know it, my restraints are loosened, and once more, I feel a hot splash of liquid in my face.

"AHHHHHHHHHHH!" I scream. "What the hell was that for?!"

The men are laughing. "Ah, nothin'! We just love seeing you react to it is all!" one of them chortles.

In a swift motion, I am whisked down a hallway. I am wholly unable to see anything, and the burning is so beyond painful that it makes me throw up by dry heaving, and start to question my level of consciousness.

I can't see anything, but I presume I am in front of the door. I hear keys jangling, the lock clicking, and feet shuffling past me. Then the lock clicks, and I am forced onto what feels like a medical examination table. As my eyes slowly begin to become less painful, I become aware that it's dark in this room. Of course, that last splash could have just been the nail in the coffin, and my eyes are toast. I could be blind.

I don't have time to think about it before I hear one of their sinister voices. *"Hey Ray."*

"What is this?"

"Oh, just you wait and see. You got good lung capacity, kid?"

Just what is this guy going to do? I've smoked a few times, but he can't know that. I have a feeling whatever this is has something to do with holding my breath, or at worst, drowning. But, I just pray I'm wrong.

Before I can think any further, I feel something wet and hard smash up against my mouth. Whatever it is, it catches me so off guard, I don't even have a chance to take in a deep breath. I squirm and fight as best as I can, but my arms are strapped. My legs are free, though, and finally, after I feel like I'm about to lose consciousness, I manage to land a good kick on the guy holding the rag to my face.

Taking a deep gasp for a breath, to my surprise, I hear the guy laughing. Right at that moment, the lights turn on. My poor pupils just can't catch a break today.

It's Jeff who is cackling at my expense. Looking around, I see nothing but metal walls, and a door. There are dozens of very large buckets full of water all over the floor.

"Know what it is yet?!" he shouts. I'm still dying from not having any air for what felt like forever, so I'm not quick enough to answer.

"It's WATERBOARDING, baby! If you can survive 10 minutes of this, or five rounds, whatever comes first, then you can move on to the NEXT room! But, be warned...I'm not going to take it easy on you the next few times!"

My insides drop like a rock inside of me. If I make it out of this alive, it will be nothing short of a miracle. Truly, I don't know if I'll ever want to drink water again after this.

Before I can even register what is happening, again, I feel the cloth crushed up against my face. Internally, I start to panic. I have never known what it's like to be scared, until I quite literally cannot breathe. As they pour the bucket over the cloth, the fire in my lungs burns white hot. I look up, and Jeff is laughing. Panicking more and more with each passing second, I kick as hard as I can, back and forth - to no avail. I start to see what my science teacher told us about one time - when you are close to death, your brain has a supercharge of electrical activity, where you see your life flash before your eyes. There is no doubt in my mind, this is what I'm experiencing. Images of my sisters, my brother, several friends, my parents, and yes, the Morrison family - all dance before my eyes.

Right when I think I'm about to die and it feels like my lungs are a tenth of a second away from bursting, he pulls the cloth away.

Gasping this breath of air is the most beautiful thing I have ever experienced in my entire life. Sputtering water out of my mouth, Jeff is laughing, already set to go with his next bucket of water. I think to myself, it surely HAS to be ten minutes by now, right? Although, I can't say I am looking forward to what's going to happen next...

Four minutes down, sport. Six to go!

Oh, good heavens. My lungs are going to be so beyond damaged.

Without any warning, Jeff starts in on me again, but he doesn't quit surprising me. This time, there isn't a cloth put onto my face. This time, Jeff and Bill work together to torture me. Bill holds my hands and feet to make sure I can't move, and Jeff starts pouring water all over my face.

At first, it isn't bad. He pours slowly, and I manage to drink at least some of it. But then, he starts to pick up speed. Suddenly, there is too much water flowing for me to breathe through my nose, and I can't escape inhaling the water with my mouth no matter which way I turn.

"LET'S GOOOOOO!" shouts either Bill or Jeff.

My lungs are on fire again. It burns and hurts like hell on wheels. Truly, it feels like I am going to drown. I cannot breathe. I cannot breathe...I cannot...

It stops. At long, long, long last, ten minutes are up.

I can't move. My heart is all erratic. I try to kick my legs at them but my brain isn't communicating anything to my body right now. Truly, this was awful.

Helping me up, Jeff asks me a question. "Ready for what's next? I don't think you are. Lots of luck to you, buster." He gives me a shove, right into the tender predations of John and Joe. My legs nearly collapse from under me, but they finally start to work again even though they feel like spaghetti.

Still reeling from almost dying, my legs about to give out, they force me to walk me down the hallway, and park me in front of another door. "What do you think's in there, twerp?" One of them asks. "Go on, three guesses." One of them grabs the nape of my shirt as he does so.

What the hell do I say to them? This is repugnant. "A gun for me to kill myself?" I ask them sarcastically, still out of breath. Tightening the grip on my shirt, they laugh, but shortly after say "nope. Try again."

I'm at a loss here. "A rope that I'm about to be whipped with?"

"Hmm, getting closer," Jeff says. One more guess, and then I'm going to be left at the mercy of whatever is behind this door. What could he mean, I'm close when I guessed a rope?

"Um...a chain you're going to hit me with."

More guffaws of laughter. Before I know it, they shove me onto the floor. The room is lighter than the last one. There is even what looks to be an egress window up toward the ceiling. Could this help me? I also notice what looks to be a clothes hamper in the middle of the floor. These guys are insane.

"You're a pretty piss poor guesser, kid. You know, originally, we thought we'd bring you in here to torture out of you just where you put our money. But now, I think we're all having too much fun watching you take this stuff on." He laughs like a jackass as he walks toward the door. Before he leaves, he tells me what I'm about to experience.

"When you said 'rope,' you were close in that you are going to be up against something long, and thin."

He directs my attention to the hamper in the middle of the room, where he walks. Pointing at it, he says, "in there, you're about to meet a Western Diamondback Rattlesnake. It's one of the most aggressive snakes in the United States, and this one is certainly no exception. If he bites you, you'll know it. You won't die right away, but the venom works slowly and painfully. If you don't get help within a few days, you'll die slowly and painfully. If you can take it out without being bit, you win. We'll let you go without going in the last door. But if you take it out after getting bit, then let's see how well the third door goes for you after you've been weakened by the snake."

Joe and John laugh like hyenas. Now, it's time.

All the while they were talking, I was thinking of something fast. Fortunately for me, when they started describing the snake, I was plotting my move. Here goes nothing.

Rushing like a madman with every ounce of strength I can muster, I run straight at John - with adrenaline pumping through my veins, I have a strength unlike anything I've ever felt before.

Before he even knows what hit him, I slam him to the ground. Hitting away his arms as hard as I can, I make a fast move and use my legs to tip the hamper over. Sure enough, I hear a hiss and a rattle, and the snake comes barreling out and lands about five feet away from us. Joe, who started to go after us, stops at the sight of the snake, who is now angrier than a bear with a trap on its foot.

John is hollering and hitting me, right as my surge of adrenaline starts to wear off. Thinking fast, I try shoving my thumbs into his eyelids, and he lets out a shrill, ungodly scream unlike anything I have ever heard. I'm sure by now we've drawn attention to somebody on the outside - certainly on the outside of this room. There were four men total - Joe and John are in here. Where are the other two? I doubt they're still in the room with the water.

Finally, my moment on the winning end comes to a halt. Grabbing me by the neck, I have a strong feeling that John is about to snap my neck and be done with me, and it will be lights out, and I will see Mom again. But, all he does is grab me, and punch me in the face so hard, that my nose immediately erupts like a volcano, and my eye starts to swell shut.

"You got some nerve, kid..." he says as he walks toward me, squinting and bleeding from his eyes. I shuffle away from him on the ground. I have lost track of the snake, but I can tell that Joe has left.

"You don't know who you're up against," I say, sounding a lot cockier than I feel. "I killed a guy on the Iowa border a few weeks ago. You don't want to mess with me."

"Oh, is that so?" he quips back. Moving closer to me, he kicks me as hard as he can, and for the next two minutes, he wails on me. I want to scream out, holler in agony - but I don't want to give him the satisfaction. Besides, the world seems lighter, now. I am seeing stars, everything is hazy, and I can't hear as well. I can feel myself starting to lose consciousness.

He only stops when I hear him cry out in pain. From my one good eye, I see him grab his leg, as my consciousness slowly starts to come back. Gradually, the snake comes back into focus as the door slams. Here I am, dazed and weak, about to be bitten by a rattlesnake, and die alone locked in this room in the woods where nobody will ever find my bones. If there's ever a time I have wanted my mom, or hell, even my dad, it's now.

.ₘₘₕ.

Slowly, and with every ounce of energy I can muster, I keep

pushing myself away from the snake. I am trying to stay out of striking range, but it keeps inching closer and closer to me. I can't help but think it's a win that certainly one, if not two of the men who brought me in here were bitten. If I remember right from the class I took on animals last year, a snake only has enough venom for two bites, which this one already may have done. Even so, I'm not willing to take the chance. I keep pushing myself away.

My thoughts are on the Morrison family. If I had just stayed with them, I wouldn't be here. This snake would be somewhere else. My thoughts also drift to my parents. I can just hear Mom saying *"fight, Ray. Fight. I'll always be with you. Fight!"* Alternatively, I can hear Dad saying *"I'm about to lose the house*

Ray. Keith could be taken away. Don't give up now. We need you."

I feel another surge of adrenaline bursting through my veins. Although still blurry and sore, I see the snake as I get to my feet. Game on.

Screaming at it louder than I did when I tackled Jeff, I run at the snake as fast as I can. As hard as I can, I kick the snake, right as I feel its teeth clip the bottom part of my leg. I know I'm bitten. Snakes are fast reactors. That doesn't stop it from flying across the room, though. The snake is not small, so I'm surprised at how far it flies.

With a thud, I hear the snake hiss something terrible, and watch as it looks to regain its orientation. I'm one step ahead of it this time, though. From how I feel right now, nobody would ever guess that I was nearly dead from waterboarding less than ten minutes ago, and had just been getting beat up on less than two minutes ago.

I kick that snake as hard as I can. I want to crush it. Kicking, stomping, and kicking some more, blood splatters across the floor and onto the walls, and finally, the snake is motionless - or what's left of it is. Victory. With the blood from the snake covering my shoes and my pants, I smile in satisfaction. They said if I can beat the snake, they'd let me go. But wait. Was that it? Did they say they'd let me go if I wasn't bitten?

Suddenly, my right foot starts to feel really tingly. It's the venom. I know I'm on borrowed time here.

Limping all the way back to the door, I notice something - and pick it up off the floor. I didn't notice this before. It must have fallen out of Joe or John's pocket during the scuffle. It's nothing short of a miracle that this is on the floor. I just know it will come in handy later. I highly doubt they'll let me out now that at least one of their men has been hurt. They didn't expect me to put up a fight. Well, Raynold Penfield has a good fighter in him. Nothing is going to take me down that easily. Not my father. Not a kidnapper. Not a car accident. Not a swarm of fire ants. Not a bunch of thugs. Not waterboarding. Not a damn rattlesnake. And NOT whatever the remaining guys have left for me. *Bring it on, bastards.*

⌇⌇⌇

At the door, amazingly it's open. Evidently, whoever had left me last was in such a hurry to get out that he left the door open.

Suddenly, I am grabbed by the back of my shirt. Before I even know what's happening, two of the men rip my shirt off of my body, and proceed to tie it around my neck.

"You've caused us a lot of trouble, kid. Joe and John had to take off to find help. You had better hope they find it, or I'll be sure to send your family pieces of you from time to time." Bill practically snarls into my ear.

I can't breathe with this around my neck. The more I struggle, the tighter he pulls. Summoning up whatever adrenaline my brain has left inside it, I try to push him away. Right as I do this, he shoves me into the last room, and slams the door. Gasping for breath, I fall to the floor. It's dark, I can't see anything, but I hear a low growl. "What the hell is that?" I ask myself. I am shaking my shoes. It sounds like an animal I don't want to meet.

Suddenly, I am stunned with a flash of white-hot, blinding light, right as an ear-splitting roar explodes in my brain. Instinctually, I move away from the noise as my eyes adjust to the bright light. Finally, I start to make out the shape of something dark, round, tall, fierce, and loud - but it quickly disappears again.

This room is by far the biggest of the three I've been in so far. Oddly enough, it looks like a library, with blocks resembling bookshelves all over the floor. Hiding behind one, I am petrified as I seek out the creature that made the most terrifying noise I have heard since the guttural screams from the psycho who was intent on taking me to Mexico. I feel another pang of pain start to crawl up my leg. The rattlesnake venom is spreading, I just know it. I need to get out of this, and fast.

Suddenly, there it is. Charging at me from around one of the large blocks, I see a large black bear. Standing on its hind legs, it roars again, ready to inflict some damage.

In an instant, the bear swipes its paw at me and I fall to the ground. How am I still alive after all of my injuries?

Thinking back to the previous room, I reach into my pocket. It's a miracle that I found this. A letter opener. A freaking letter opener. Why the hell was this in his pocket? Anybody's guess is as good as mine.

Wielding my only weapon as the pain surges further up my leg, I take a few stabs at the bear. I have adrenaline surging through my veins, but I've taken several blows to the head, so I can't be seeing straight. The bear continues to swipe at and roar at me, and soon enough, I see its head start to head for my neck.

Throwing my arms up to shield my throat, the bear sinks its teeth into my arms. It feels like a giant vice with teeth has clamped itself onto me; and there's no way to release it. In the struggle, I make the crucial mistake of dropping my only weapon. It lays on the ground about three feet from me. If I could just get one arm free...

In a split second, the bear readjusts its grip on my arm and I seize on the opportunity. Yanking my left arm free, I reach across my body and reach desperately for the weapon on my right side. The bear is just crushing my legs and pelvis. One silver lining is that he may be suppressing the venom from traveling further up my leg for the time being.

I feel myself getting weaker, and weaker, and weaker. Time is traveling in slow motion right now. Is this *finally* the end? I find myself suddenly filled with an immense amount of sadness. This is how my life will end. I'm going to die right here on the floor of a renovated warehouse in the middle of some woods, where nobody will ever find what's left of me after this monster finishes devouring my flesh.

Suddenly, I see an even brighter light - which is a difficult feat given how bright it is in here right now. But as the light I see gets brighter, the room becomes dimmer. The bear still has an iron-clad grip on my right arm, but it's suddenly like he has frozen.

What comes next shocks me. Riding down on the light, I see my mother. Smiling at me, she holds out her arm and points a finger at me, with her other arm on her hip. Am I going crazy? Is that Elvis music I hear in the background?

"Don't give up, Ray. Reach with all your might!" she says.

"I can't, Mother! He's too strong!"

"You have everything you need. Reach, son. Reach!"

Reaching with all my might, summoning every ounce of strength I can muster, I feel what must be my shoulder muscle tearing as I finally am able to grab the weapon. In that split second, Mother is gone – and I'm back to where I was just before.

Screaming at the top of my lungs at the bear – who at this point is covered in slobber and tons of my blood – I grip the letter opener in the mangled fingers of my left hand and sink the blade into its eye.

Pressing as hard as I can, I listen as the bear howls in pain and immediately recoils. But that doesn't stop me. Following it, I keep pushing. I won't stop until the damn thing has pierced his brain.

I wrestle with it, keeping the weapon in its eye as it thrashes. Suddenly, the bear goes limp and twitches, as blood pools around its head.

Taking stock of my injuries, I see that the bear has done an unbelievable amount of damage to my arms - one of which was just starting to recover after the car accident. Still, better my arms than my throat. My torso is shredded and gashed, but fortunately no ribs seem to be broken, and I can breathe okay, which is a miracle, considering I've been both choked and waterboarded.

The Roamer

It hurts like hell to move and try to stand, but it appears that my pelvis has survived. My leg is turning a weird shade of purple, and it is starting to burn like a fire. I need a doctor, as fast as possible. I know I can't last more than a few days on a rattlesnake bite. The men are right; my blood will become poisoned and eventually turn to jelly. What a painful way to go.

I need to get out. Making sure I still have the letter opener, I make my way to the door, stepping over the dead bear as I do so.

"HEY! PSYCHOS! I BEAT YOUR CHALLENGES! NOW LET ME GO!"

Jeff and Bill, the water boarders, walk down the now bright hallway as if they can't believe I'm still here. I feel like James Bond. I don't read a lot of books, but that one I have. I feel like the total

147

badass that James Bond is, considering what I've just accomplished.

Looking at each other when they reach me, it's clear they hadn't planned for this. They don't know what to do. They were expecting me to die in there.

"Let. Me. Go," I snarl, starting to sound more like the bear. My fist grips around the handle of the letter opener, and I feel in my pocket, the other stink bomb I got from the store when I was with Matthew. I must bide my time. These are my only defenses. But if they try to kill me, I'll fight them. They won't be able to breathe with this thing in their face, and it may be just enough to distract them so I can escape. But if that isn't enough, I have learned that I have the fighting spirit of an animal right now - if I've survived all of this for this long, I'm not about to give up without a fight. I'm doing it for Mother.

The men just chuckle. Crossing their arms, with a sinister tone, they say, "let's hope you're a good swimmer, kid."

Oh, no they don't. Smiling, I let off the stink bomb, and, right as it explodes, I throw it in Bill's face. Right as he cries out, I grip the letter opener, and swing it at Bill's neck like somebody with a switchblade in an old movie. I didn't make as good of a connection as I had hoped to, due to how bad my arms hurt from the bear.

He makes a grab for his neck, and bolts down the hallway for the door, right as Jeff knocks me over. Raising his fist, he goes for my head. He's aiming for the kill, I just know it. Raising my one good leg, I aim for the spot that every man dreads being kicked. I land my blow with a satisfying thud against his pelvis.

Grunting and staggering backwards, I raise the weapon I used to kill the bear. Right as he barrels toward me, I instinctively put my hands up to protect my face. Only this time, the blood-stained blade of the weapon they had intended to use on me is angled directly at his head. With shock and awe, I watch as Jeff's eye is impaled by the letter opener in a near identical way that the bear's was. The rest is all a blur. I'm up and out of there as fast as I can.

Listening to a grown man's agonizing screams is more petrifying and haunting than anything I've ever heard in my entire life.

I have to get out of here. My leg is in real danger of killing me and my arms will develop an infection if I don't find help soon. The other guys may still be out there, so I have to watch my every step.

After finding an open door that the first two guys must have used to escape after their snake bites, I stumble blindly through the woods. It's dark, blurry, hazy, and back to freezing. Damn snow. How far north did they take me? I have a feeling I'm somewhere back in Minnesota, though. I collapse into the snow when I am finally out of sight from the warehouse of horrors.

Finally - after all this time - the dam breaks loose. I start to cry. This whole fiasco has finally caught up with me. I had been within seconds of death one too many times. My mother had saved me - I really believe that. Everything I have been bottling up about her finally comes spilling out into the blood and tear soaked snow. Everything from regret of not being there when she died, the trouble I got into at school and how she would hate me for it, to fighting with my father and running away from home and getting myself into a mess like this. Damned if anybody sees me right now - I couldn't care less.

Hyper-aware of any danger that may be around me, I seek shelter. My leg feels hot and numb, and feels comparable to how your foot feels when it comes back to life after it has fallen asleep - only on a much larger scale, with pain that never stops. By now the pain is up to my thigh, and by morning, it's bound to be in my groin.

Through it all, I pull myself into an alcove of trees that offers some shelter from the elements, and hopefully, from the much greater threat of the men who tried to kill me.

As I lay there, I look up at the stars and think to myself, just why on earth would those guys want to kill me, again? This was the most bizarre twist to my story. They thought I was somebody else who had stolen money from their gang or from them. Well, I may not have stolen anything from them, however, I am guilty of stealing my mother's heart. I finally drift off to a limited state of sleep, knowing that she did indeed love me.

Chapter Eight

I wake up in agonizing pain. It's still dark. I'm tired, I'm thirsty, I'm hungry, and I don't want to be on this journey anymore. I would take an eternity with my dad over this hell anyday, now.

My leg is just about useless. I can't bear any weight on it anymore. Dragging myself over snow on my way toward a creek running through the woods, I drink until I feel like I'm about to puke. Water has never tasted so good in my whole entire life. It's cold, refreshing, and gives me another burst of energy.

I have no idea how I survived the night. These injuries are horrific, and it is still freezing out here. My arms have deep wounds in them, from the bear's teeth. The venom from the rattler hasn't spread to my groin yet, but if I don't keep with it, I'll be paralyzed or dead in no time. My vision isn't improving by any stretch. Probably from the vinegar with pepper juice they threw into it early on, or being hit in the face so many times, it's swollen shut. Or some combination of both.

Pushing forward, I find a large branch that allows me to stand and hobble forward without putting too much weight on the leg that has been damaged by venom. Make no mistake, I still hurt like hell, but this is a welcome relief. I can cover more ground this way. I *need* to make it out of these woods if I want a chance at saving my leg.

At long last, I finally make it out of the woods just as the sun peeks over the horizon. Even though my vision is still cloudy, it is just the most beautiful and rejuvenating experience I have ever had. I am spurred onward by the thought of any of those clowns that may catch up with me after this. I need to get home, and report them to the police so they can't do this to anyone else. What a bizarre brush with death that was.

By mid-morning, I finally manage to find the road, just in time for a break. They must have traveled quite a ways with me to get me into that insane warehouse. That thought haunts my mind and freaks me out. *How long was I* unconscious? *What did they do to me while I was out?* I can't think about it too much. I'm exhausted, cold, and in so, so, so much pain. I just want this to be over with.

When I feel ready to go again, I hit the road. I don't know where I am going, but I stick to the road that is heading north. I am on borrowed time with this leg, and my time will soon run out.

Suddenly, up ahead, is a sight that will forever be etched into my memories. In an instant, my heart drops to my stomach and shatters. I can't believe this is real. Can't. Freaking. Believe. It.

Peering over the edge of a bridge down a ravine, I see a camper. But it's not sitting upright. It has a crushed front, and it's upside down.

Nobody has to ask me twice, I know exactly what camper that is.

Upon looking closer, I see their van. Broken. Crashed. Destroyed.

Internal panic sets in. My scream of horror echoes down the bridge.

Forgetting the stick, I begin to barrel down the ravine toward the wreckage. Losing my balance, I tumble and fall, coming within inches of fatally striking my head against a rock.

Down here, I can hear faint, but weak cries. "Help."

"Help!"

I hear Wayne and Julie for sure. But no sign of Matthew. Limping around to the back, I see that Wayne was partially ejected by the vehicle and has had his leg crushed by the van, and can't get out. "RAYNOLD!" he shouts as lively as he can, but still weak. Taking my hands, he pleads with me. "Please. We need help. Julie's trapped inside! No sign of Matthew. Hurry, please!"

This amount of adrenaline can't be healthy for a human brain. But my brain is flooded with it once again. My arms are still just about worthless. Wasting no time, I find another large branch and place it under the edge of the car. Throwing my whole body weight against it, the end of the vehicle lifts maybe two inches above the ground for maybe three seconds. It's just enough time for him to rapidly pull backwards and free his leg.

"AHHH!" he screams. If I thought my body looked bad, his leg was ten times worse. I would be amazed if he stood a chance at walking again after this, no pun intended.

He's free. Now Julie. Using the same branch to shatter the window on the overturned van, I see Julie, unconscious, on the passenger seat, which happens to be closest to the ground right now. "JULIE!" I scream, "WE NEED TO GET OUT OF HERE!" No movement. Oh no.

Grabbing some water from a nearby creek, I throw it down onto her. Jolting awake, I breathe a sigh of relief. After recognizing me, she reaches up toward the branch, and manages to climb up through the window. Wayne is on the ground, moaning in pain from his shattered leg, but Julie seems mostly unscathed other than maybe a concussion, which is a miracle.

"RAY!" I hear a voice call out. Turning around, I see Matthew, coming toward us from upstream. Throwing himself at me, I start to cry all over again, as does he.

"We saw those guys take you! We took off after them, then we crashed! I left to find help, and now here you are!"

Julie wraps us both up in a hug, and for a second, I really believe we are safe. "Let's get out of here," I say. "We are all on borrowed time, let's go."

"Oh, no you don't," a voice says from up the ravine.

Looking up, my heart sinks. Joe and John from the warehouse are making their way toward us, guns drawn. Looking down, I see that John has a bandage on his leg, indicating John has recovered from the snake, and Joe found him help. Jeff is dead, Bill is nowhere to be found. *Oh no.*

"You put us up to a lot of trouble, kid. And now you've seen our faces. I think there's only one way to settle this." John cocks his gun and points it at my head.

Matthew, feeling the obvious need to defend me, runs at the attackers, taking Joe by such surprise, he falls onto the ground. This happens right as John strikes me in the head with a large rock, and everything goes dark. The last thing I remember hearing is Wayne shouting "NO!"

Chapter Nine

Oh boy. Now where am I? I wake up laying on my back, and I can't get up. The world is hazy, and it feels as if I am teetering on a knife's edge of life. My head feels heavy, and my vision is very poor.

I can't talk. I have tubes coming in and out of my throat. My arms are tethered high above my head, wrapped in what feels like a giant cast.

I hear somebody talking. "I think he's awake!"

The bed is adjusted so I can see who is talking. Slowly, I make out the shapes of Wayne, Julie, and Matthew, who all start to cry. Wayne is in a wheelchair with a full cast on his leg, Julie is bent over me in tears, and Matthew stands next to his mother, waiting for his turn at my bedside.

"Ray. You saved our lives. It was nothing short of a God-ordained miracle that you found us when you did, Ray. You are our hero!"

Of course, I can't respond, but I close my eyes and try to smile to let her know that I heard her. More than anything, I want to tell her in no uncertain terms just how important her family is to me, and how truly, they were the ones who saved *my* life on this trip, in more ways than one. But all of that stays inside my head. I couldn't get the words out if I tried due to exhaustion.

Like a magician's trick, a doctor comes into the room and starts talking to me. He tells me how I was darn near death when I was brought in. Head trauma almost took my life. They had to work hard to save my leg, and I would likely have some long lasting problems with it. He says I was likely to develop neuropathy in one or both of my feet as I get older, as a result of the damaged nerves from the venom. Whatever neuropathy is, I'll worry about it later. I'm just thankful to have both of my legs still with me.

He also went on to say that I have severe head trauma from being hit with a rock, and my eyesight will not be as strong, thanks to the vinegar and pepper they threw into my face. My arms were nearly a lost cause. He nearly didn't believe it when he heard I had lifted a vehicle off of Wayne's broken leg with arms like that. He said he is curious as to what kind of animal did the damage, but he knows I can't answer right now.

"All in all, you are a very lucky kid, Raynold. You were there for this family when they needed you. Now let's get that tube out of your mouth so you can talk to them."

After some pulling and some gagging, the tube was free, and I could finally tell my friends exactly how glad I am to see them. Oh, to heck with friends. They are my bonus family now.

My voice is weak. Hoarsely, I say "How did you get free? The last thing I remember is seeing them coming down the hill with a gun,

Matthew charging them, and then everything went dark."

They tense up, and I can't blame them. It has to be incredibly traumatic reliving what they probably are right now.

"The second you were knocked out, they nearly killed Matthew. But we said we'd give them whatever they wanted, so we paid them a ransom. Then they left, and shortly after, we were spotted by a police car, who called for an ambulance. If he hadn't come by at that moment, I have a feeling we wouldn't be sitting here talking right now."

My chest feels like it's about to explode. Son of a gun. Those bastards really were after money.

"How much did they take from you?" I ask, incensed that they were scared into paying ransom in their highest moment of need.

"It doesn't matter," Wayne says. "We paid it, and it's over. We have you, and we have Matthew. You are going to be fine, and it looks like we all are. That's all that matters."

And that's that. But, they have more surprises up their sleeves.

"Ray, we have a surprise for you," Julie says. She motions to the door.

I am stunned. In walks my father, my two sisters, Mary Lynn and Jane, and Keith. The sight of me makes my sisters cry, and I swear I even see the glint of a tear in my father's eye.

"Hope you're ready to come home, son," Dad grunts, trying to force back tears.

I draw in a deep breath. "I am ready to come home."

My family surrounds me, and gives me a hug, while the Morrison family looks on.

"We were able to touch base with your father not long before we got here," Julie says. "They traveled a long way to come here."

Dad nods. "I have good news too, Ray," he says. Curious, I listen on.

"Your mother's surgeon has done something incredible for our family. He has personally wiped away all of our debt from your mother's surgery. We don't owe a penny on it anymore. All that's left is the debt from her time in the hospital, which I can pay off a lot easier over time. We can keep the house, and Keith is here to stay."

My heart is soaring. How can so much luck be on my side? It just has to be God. A higher power is the only explanation I have for all of this. God is watching out for my family.

"What a blessing," I say. Dad actually smiles. My sisters wipe away tears. Keith stands there staring at me, marveling at all of my bandages, casts, and tubes.

A random thought hits me in the middle of the family love fest.

"What happened to the guys who did most of the damage to me? Did the police find the bear and the snake?"

Dad, my sisters, and Keith all give each other weird looks, as if they think I must have gotten hit hard in the head.

Wayne and Julie look my way. After a short pause, they give me a long, measuring look.

"One of them is gone, Ray. But the two who took our money, plus what they think is one more, they escaped. The police haven't seen any trace of them since they fled. But rest assured, you will be kept safe."

I try to believe that, but pangs of anxiety echo all throughout my body. For the rest of my life, until those goons are caught, I will forever remain haunted by the crazy psychopaths who did this to me. But, I have to admit, it says a lot that I've met five psychos on this journey, and two of them are dead, while I'm alive.

"Almost forgot to tell you," Wayne says. "You left your trombone behind when you left the camper." Regrettably, I don't have it with me right now, but amazingly, it was one of the few things that didn't get damaged too badly when the camper crashed. I guess you'll have to come by our house sometime to pick it up."

"YEAH!" says Matthew, clearly excited.

I smile, ready for an adventure as soon as I get out of here. "That sounds like it will work!" My sisters, brother, and father all smile, along with the entire Morrison family. I survived the biggest nightmare of my entire life. But, I'm a survivor. I'm fit for the military. I'm ready for just about anything. Game on. Adventure is out there.

Made in the USA
Middletown, DE
26 August 2024

59309575R00106